How to Kill
A Murderer

How to Kill a Murderer

Nicholas S. Sorrenti

Library of Congress Control Number: 2017915693
ISBN: Hardcover   978-1-5434-5755-1
     Softcover   978-1-5434-5756-8
     eBook   978-1-5434-5757-5

Print information available on the last page.

Rev. date: 10/14/2017

To order additional copies of this book, contact:
Xlibris
1-888-795-4274
www.Xlibris.com
Orders@Xlibris.com
767982

CONTENTS

ACKNOWLEDGMENT

I want to thank those who have taught me valuable lessons throughout the journey of writing my book. There comes a point in life where you must take a leap of faith and put yourself into a position to succeed. With limited resources, you have to take full advantage of opportunities that may arise, even if these opportunities are self-made.

To answer the question regarding what inspired me to write a book, all I could honestly say is the truth. A simple topic in one of my previous college history courses sparked an idea that developed into an idea and now a published book.

Lastly, I want to thank not only a true friend but also a loving and selfless yet determined human being for pushing me to pursue my dream of publishing my first book. Ryan, you have become someone that continues to push me to become the best person and entrepreneur that I can be. Never lose sight of your goals and continue to help others achieve theirs.

CHAPTER 1

Foreshadow

With the warm yet bitter taste of his freshly splattered blood on the tip of my tongue, I did not understand what had just happened. The emotional imbalance that had taken over my body within a split second was something I have never endured. What do I do? How do I fix this? Who do I call? These questions began racing through my mind at an uncontrollable rate. Something had to be done.

As the muted courtroom became filled with screams and unknown suspicion, I noticed three police officers running toward me. While still being in shock, I began to think they were coming to help me, but as they pushed me aside and grabbed the lifeless yet loved body on the ground, the death of my best friend became real.

CHAPTER 2

Almost Perfect

The Shaww family lived in Brooksville, Long Island, a very wealthy, upper middle-class, all-white neighborhood. The Shawws were not prodigious by any means; however, this is what the neighborhood consisted of.

The Shawws are a highly respected family throughout their neighborhood and well-known due to Mr. Shaww, also referred to as Jeff, winning a historic court case in Long Island, dating back to 1999. The Shaww family had four total members, including Jeff. The three additional members are Bonnie and two identical twins, Connor and Parker. Even though, as a family, the Shawws seemed picture-perfect, both Jeff and Bonnie did not experience perfect childhoods.

Bonnie, as a child, witnessed a family that was extremely separated. With her parents being divorced and her brother and sister coming in and out of her life, she promised herself that when the day came that she had a family of her own, she would do everything in her power to make her children and husband feel safe and, most importantly, loved. Due to her childhood, she had to grow up faster than most kids her age, which resulted in her transitioning into an a independent woman consisting of extremely strong qualities, such as being a caregiver, wanting the best for everyone, and always putting others before herself.

With these qualities becoming a staple to Bonnie's personality, it led to her wanting to direct her focus toward being an education teacher. She received her certification to teach grades K–5, and this type of lifestyle had given her nothing but joy and happiness. As a mother, Bonnie, like many good mothers, would do anything for her children. She always made sure to put her two boys first and to help them with anything they may be going through. The people that had a relationship with Bonnie knew she is truly a genuine person and kindhearted individual.

With the many blessings that both Jeff and Bonnie had experienced throughout their marriage, their biggest accomplishment was the birth of their two boys, Connor and Parker. These boys are inseparable. Even though Parker is only a minute and a half older, they both treated each other as equals and, surprisingly, with respect at all times. With this being said, this did not mean that their lives were perfect.

With Parker being the more athletically gifted twin and being ranked the top baseball player in his class, it resulted in him having more friends. Connor, however, was not as fortunate. Connor was more of the intellectual, highly intelligent, somewhat nerdy teenage boy. Even though Parker would always include Connor in things, Parker knew that he did not fit in with his group of friends. Even though this was obvious in both twins' eyes, Connor wanted to hang with Parker at all times, so he always made sure to say yes whenever Parker asked him to hang out with him and the guys.

From the outside perspective, the Shawws' neighbors viewed them as the modern-day Brady Bunch. However, within the Shawws' household, things will begin to quickly change once Mr. Shaww breaks some devastating news to the family.

In the past, the Shawws' home was known as the community hangout. They would always have friends and family over on the weekends. From the minute someone walked in to the minute they left, people were socializing, music was playing, games were being played, and in the words of Bonnie Shaww, "they were creating one memory at a time."

With the first quarter of the middle school marking period coming to an end for Connor and Parker, they both began to get excited for the holidays. Christmas was just a few days away, and they knew what type of things came with Christmas. It was not just the gifts but also the annual Christmas Eve party that the Shawws have made a tradition over the past thirteen years. The entire neighborhood would come—, friends, family, pets, everything, and& everyone.

However, even though the Christmas Eve party was something the boys always looked forward to, Connor and Parker were still two thirteen-year-olds who were ecstatic about their Christmas list. Connor wanted a new computer, as well as some baseball equipment. Parker ironically asked for baseball equipment as well. One thing that did surprise Bonnie and Jeff was the fact that Parker asked for a black journal. Bonnie and Jeff didn't understand why he wanted a journal, but Parker made it clear that he just wanted to write down his goals, as well as his baseball statistics for this upcoming season.

Soon enough, Christmas was in the air:; the smell of fresh ginger bread coming out of the oven, and the beautiful site of bright lights, dark- green wreaths covered with red ribbons, and the most intriguing of them all, the enormous number of presents under the Shawws' eight-foot Christmas tree.

On the night of Christmas Eve, the Shaww household was packed and exhilarating as ever. As dinnertime came near, Jeff and Bonnie took control of the room by chiming their champagne glasses to make a toast.

With all champagne glasses in the room being raised and several tears running down Bonnie's cheeks, the room became desolate. The only thing being heard was the ice stirring around the silver bucket filled with soda and alcoholic beverages.

With Mrs. Shaww becoming overwhelmed with emotion, Mr. Shaw took over.

"I just want to make it clear to everyone that we love and care about all of you very much and we want to thank you all for coming out here this evening to make this Christmas Eve a memorable one. With that being said, Mrs. Shaww and I have some news. I was offered a position at a law firm in New York City, and Bonnie and I have agreed that it would not only be a great opportunity for myself but, importantly, our family if I were to take this position."

After this was said, the room began to fill with joy. Their friends and family began congratulating the Shawws. However, Mr. and Mrs. Shaww knew that their neighbors did not understand what Mr. Shaww was trying to say. Jeff understood this and stopped the commotion.

As he tapped the champagne glass a little harder, Jeff explained, "I don't believe all of you understand what I am saying. Yes, this news is wonderful, and we are very excited and blessed as a family to have this opportunity, but with this change in jobs, this also means that we will have to move to New York."

Friends and family that were smiling and overjoyed less than a minute ago became silent and nonresponsive. This toast sucked the life out of the room. It was a harsh environment for the Shawws, but it seemed as though the two individuals who took the news the hardest were Connor and Parker.

Both were in the corner of the room, looking at each other with eyes full of fear, knowing things were about to change. They both knew it would soon become a change that they both would have to adjust to. But with this move, they both understood that they had to be there for each other no matter what.

With the party ending and Christmas morning within sight, Connor and Parker began talking in Parker's room. He and Connor always spent Christmas Eve night together in one of their rooms. This made them feel as if they were little kids again—the type of feeling that consisted of butterflies in their stomachs while waiting for Santa to make his way to their house. As one could tell, Connor and Parker are both young and innocent teenage boys that have been confined and practically brainwashed within an environment that would soon change drastically.

As they began crawling into bed, tucking themselves into Parker's Derek Jeter blanket, they began talking. As one conversation led to the next, they both began speaking about the possibility of good things coming out of this move. They tried to state the pros and cons throughout their conversation, and as the conversation unfolded, it seemed as though they were getting a better feeling about this move. They spoke about their previous visits to the city and how they loved the fast-paced environment consisting of the yellow taxies, the continuous sound of car horns being honked, and their favorite part, the mile-high skyscrapers.

Even though their visits to the city were always extremely different from the environment they experienced in Brooksville, they believed that if they stood together, they could make this move work. Connor, however, was still a little skeptical about the whole thing due to many reasons. Parker could see that and explained to Connor, "I know you're stressin' about this still, but in all actuality, this might be good for us. We'll be around different types of kids, and I bet there's a ton of talent down there for baseball." Connor, however, didn't have something like baseball to look forward to. He knew he would still be the outsider people looked at, unlike Parker, due to his baseball abilities. Connor explained in a low and scared voice.

Connor explained in a low and scared voice, "Yeah, maybe it'll be good for you, but I'm gonna be lost. I just started making friends, and it's the eighth grade, and with high school being here, even if we stayed in Brooksville, I would have to make friends all over again. Now I'm really not going to know anybody."

Tears began coming out of Connor's eyes. Parker felt for Connor, but he knew that Connor needed to grow up and start interacting with kids. Parker told Connor, "Listen, man, if you promise to go into this move with open arms, I promise to introduce you to every new person I meet, but you have to promise."

Connor replied, "I promise, man, but you better keep your word." As time unfolded, the conversations became shorter, and their breathing became heavier, and within an hour, the boys were fast asleep.

Christmas morning was here, and so were the gifts. With Connor and Parker waking up with a room full of presents, it took their minds off the move. Connor received three new books and a new computer, which was not very common for a thirteen-year-old in the year 2000.

After Connor received the computer, Parker knew that this move was planned for a while and that this was how Mr. and Mrs. Shaww were trying to say sorry. Connor also got some baseball stuff that he asked for, which made him pumped up and resulted in him immediately asking if they were going to have a backyard at their new house. Bonnie responded, "Yes, but it's not very big." Immediately Connor's face saddened, but Parker chimed in and said, "Don't worry, man, we'll make do with what we have. I'm sure there's a park somewhere around our area. I'll teach you a thing or two." Connor gave Parker a grin, but Parker knew that meant a lot to Connor.

However, in the back of Connor's head, Connor knew that he couldn't be selfish and needed to understand that Parker was probably going through some of his own emotional changes about this move. And because of that, Connor wanted to do his best to try to be strong for Parker, and so he pulled out the gift that he bought for Parker.

Parker began unwrapping, and it was the black journal. Parker was pumped, and Connor knew he got him the right gift. Connor looked at Parker and began laughing. "I was thinking about getting you a bigger book because now you're gonna have to write down my stats too, but I figured I'd save you the embarrassment and get my own journal." Parker started laughing along with Connor and thanked him with a fist pump.

Parker's gift unwrapping just began. He also received a new baseball glove, bat, and batter's helmet. And last but not least, his big gift was two third-base line tickets to go see the New York Yankees play next year. Parker jumped up in excitement and ran over to both Bonnie and Jeff, leaping onto the couch to give them both a hug.

Lastly, Bonnie and Jeff gave the boys beepers; this was so that they were able to get in contact with one another at any time of the day, as well as Bonnie and Jeff being able to reach them in such a hectic environment. The boys were excited about their beepers, not only because they would be able to get in touch with each other, but mainly due to them knowing that that they would immediately be known as the cool kids.

Once the presents were unwrapped and the Shawws went their separate ways until dinnertime, Connor passed by Parker's room and saw Parker writing in his book. He didn't understand why he was writing in it already other than if he was writing down his goals, but as of right now, Parker never told Connor that he had any current goals. He also didn't have any statistics to write down, so Connor was a little confused, but he still didn't feel that it was his business to ask what he was writing. In the end, Connor thought, *At least he's utilizing what I bought him.*

With that thought process, it resulted in Connor walking into Parker's room to say that he couldn't believe that this was their last Christmas in their house and that he was really going to miss it. Parker unexpectedly kept writing and nodded at Connor. Ignoring Connor was something that Parker never did, but Connor figured he was just enjoying the gift, so he slowly closed Parker's door and went back to his room.

- A few hours passed, and Bonnie yelled upstairs to the boys, "Dinner is ready!" Both Connor and Parker ran downstairs. As they came together for the last time for Christmas grace in their house, Bonnie prayed, "God, thank you for this food, my children, my loving husband, and our wonderful dog, Baxter. I hope you will continue to guide us through the next step of our lives in New York City, make t a great experience for all of us, and give us opportunities that we never would have thought was possible. Amen."

After Bonnie's prayer, conversations began, empty plates became covered, and the devouring of ham, macaroni, vegetables, and many other delicious foods began to be consumed However, the food was about the only thing that went perfect that night. Parker went from being ecstatic during the unwrapping of gifts to being extremely frustrated and somewhat nasty toward his parents during dinner.

To begin, he did not partake in the blessing of their food, he then began making loud burping gestures midway through dinner, and lastly, he started voicing off to both Mr. and Mrs. Shaww. After Parker continued with his inappropriate actions Bonnie dropped her utensils on her plate and asked Parker what was bothering him, and out of nowhere, Parker stood up in anger, kicking his chair back, and yelled out, "Everything is going to change, and Connor and I aren't too thrilled about it!" Connor stood there in confusion because he thought they were both past the negatives that might come from the move.

Bonnie stood up and explained to the boys, "I know this news is tough to swallow, but you have to try to go about your everyday routine like we're not going anywhere. You both have another six months here with your friends, and who knows, maybe we can get a summerhouse in the area and you both will be able to hang out with your friends during the summers. I'm sorry all of this is happening so fast, but I promise that you guys are gonna love the excitement and different types of people down there. We're gonna have a lot of fun, but you have to open your arms to the new area once were down there, because if you don't, nothing is going to go smoothly for any of us."

Connor and Parker both gazed at Bonnie with a look of frustration, and then Parker took off without permission; quickly after, Connor asked politely to leave the table as well. Bonnie excused Connor, and he then went into his room.

Later that night, Parker and Connor both went into the basement and sat around the game room and hung out. While they were sitting there, they heard yelling from upstairs. Parker then looked over and said, "I guess the move is getting to them too, huh?"

Sure enough, it was, but both of them did not expect that arguing was going to become a habit for the Shawws, but as the months went by, fighting was actually the only thing that became known as a normal thing for them.

The months went by faster than ever, and six months went to four months, and four months went to two months, and soon enough, the Shawws only had one month left in Brooksville.

With one month left for the boys, Bonnie decided to allow Connor and Parker to throw a going-away party. She told them that they could invite anyone that they wanted! She was hoping that this would allow the boys to enjoy themselves one last time with their friends before they moved.

That night, the Shawws decided to make a flyer on a piece of paper; this was so Bonnie would be able to go to the store the next day and make additional copies so that Connor and Parker would be able to hand them out in school. The next day came, and both Connor and Parker made an agreement not to tell anyone about the party until the official flyers were completed and they could be handed out. Both boys were looking forward to getting home after school; this was so that they can see the finished product.

On the walk home, Connor and Parker were excited and were trying to figure out what they were going to do at the party, but sadly, once they turned onto their street, they could hear yelling. Once again, this yelling was coming from their parents, and it was still a sound that they were not accustomed to or comfortable with hearing, immediately making them upset.

As they walked into the house, dropping both of their book bags to catch the attention of their parents, Bonnie and Jeff both stopped yelling. With frustration building up within Connor, he exploded and started screaming at both of his parents, "This is all you guys do now! It's so fuckin' annoying!" Bonnie, in disbelief cut Connor off, "Excuse you, Connor!"

Connor, "No, Mom, I'm sick of hearing you and Dad fight, like this move is only affecting you guys. It's affecting all of us, and by you arguing, it's not making any of this better. All Parker and I want is to enjoy the last month that we have here, and by you guys arguing, it isn't helping . . . So I'm asking you, for both me and Parker, please stop fighting." *PARKER & ME*

Connor immediately ran upstairs in frustration, and Parker stood there in silence. Bonnie told Parker, "Go upstairs and talk to your brother and tell him that we're sorry." Parker left to talk to Connor, while Bonnie and Jeff finished their argument.

Both of them tried to end their argument quickly so that it wouldn't upset the boys. They understood that this move was affecting all of them and they needed to be strong for the boys; so at the end of their argument, they made an agreement to stop their fighting. They understood that Connor was right, and by them fighting, it was only making the move harder for all of them.

Later that afternoon, Connor knocked on Parker's bedroom door expecting Parker to reply with "Come in." However, Connor did not hear anyone. Not knowing what to expect, Connor opened the door and immediately saw Parker throw something toward the corner of his room. Connor asked Parker what he just threw, but Parker played dumb and responded with "What are you talking about?" Connor, not questioning his brother, asked, "Do you want to go downstairs and check out the flyers?" Parker nodded, and they both ran down the stairs in excitement.

After seeing the flyers, they were trying to figure out when the best time of the day would be to hand out the flyers in school. With Connor being the more practical thinker, he came up with the idea of handing them out during lunchtime, since their entire eighth-grade class would be in the cafeteria.

With the next day taking off, it was almost lunchtime for the eighth-grade class. Connor and Parker were excited to hand out their flyers, and they knew that this party was going to make them remembered by all their friends in Brooksville.

Soon enough, everyone came rushing into the cafeteria, and both Connor and Parker began handing flyers out left and right. They must have handed them out to about every single one of their friends whom they saw. There was no holding back for them!

With all flyers handed out, they now began focusing on the shopping part of the party. They had to get their parents to buy everything that they wanted in order to make the party become everything they wanted it to be. They didn't see this being a problem due to Connor and Parker both knowing that their parents felt bad about the move, so they would do anything to make things a little easier for both of them.

After a few days of shopping and the last couple of days of school being nearby, the party was only a few days away. Both boys were experiencing the feeling of excitement as well as sadness. They were experiencing a bittersweet feeling because they wanted the party to be there but not moving day. Unfortunately, the days were moving fast, and before they knew it, party day was here!

With kids beginning to get dropped off, they were welcomed with a huge sign that said, *"CONNOR AND PARKER: it's not goodbye, it's 'see you later.'"* With about thirty eighth graders showing up, majority of them being Parker's friends, the house began to fill up pretty quickly; thankfully, the Shawws had a big backyard, and they also had plenty of things planned out for them to do.

In their backyard, they had a baseball field, where the boys planned for all their friends to play a baseball game. Bonnie and Jeff bought about fifteen cheap baseball gloves for the backyard, and this allowed teams to be split up evenly for both teams. Within minutes, bats began swinging, and voices began cheering!

Unexpectedly, a half hour in, the cheering that was being heard minutes before turned into chanting; however, it was now a violent chant. Parker was screaming at one of the football players that came because he was picking on Connor. Connor wasn't the best baseball player, and Parker knew that, but Connor tried hard to fit in and play the best that he could, and this football player was calling him a girl because he couldn't throw the ball far.

In the middle of all this commotion, embarrassment began sinking in, and tears began rolling out of Connor's eyes; it resulted in Connor pouting off into the outfield. This caused Parker to react in rage. With his emotions and anger building up inside over the past few months, Parker immediately yelled at Joe, the football player. With this altercation becoming physical, Joe began pushing Parker. With Parker being the physical specimen that he was for his age, he immediately tackled Joe as if he was a running back; he then got on top of Joe and began punching him repeatedly. With the chants of "Fight, fight, fight" being echoed into the Shawws' home, Bonnie and Jeff sprinted outside to break up the altercation.

With this, it resulted in Bonnie calling everyone's parents and asking them to come pick up their children. Bonnie did not feel that it would be appropriate to keep the party going after a big incident like that. Once Parker and Connor heard the news, they sprinted upstairs and locked Parker's door.

Connor was worked up and didn't know what exactly to say to Parker, but one thing he did ask was "How did you do that?" Parker wouldn't answer Connor; all he said was "Leave me alone right now, Connor." Connor knew Parker was in a bad mood and he didn't want to be bothered, but in the corner of Connor's eye, he spotted Parker's black book. Connor, in that moment, thought this might be a good time for Parker to utilize his gift to write down what he was feeling, especially since he didn't want to speak to anyone.

After seeing Parker snap the way he did on Joe, Connor figured that Parker wasn't really using the black book for baseball statistics like he claimed he would but, instead, was writing down some of the mixed emotions he was dealing with due to the move. As Connor handed Parker the black journal, Parker looked up at Connor with a grin of appreciation, as Connor nodded in return and left Parker's room.

Once everyone left, Bonnie went up to Connor's room and asked him why Parker acted out the way he did. Connor explained everything that happened, and Bonnie understood that Parker was trying to protect his brother, but from what Connor explained to her, Bonnie got the same feeling that Connor did, regarding Parker acting out the way he did due to the buildup of emotions and frustrations from this move.

With that, Bonnie walked to the next room and knocked on Parker's door, but with her not getting a quick response, she opened up the door. As the door opened, she did not see Parker. The window was open, and the only thing Bonnie saw was the white curtain blowing from the wind. She then screamed for Jeff. Immediately after, she ran into Connor's room, asking him if he knew where Parker was, and he replied by saying, "He was just on his bed a little while ago." Bonnie's stomach sank. With her mother intuition kicking in, she knew something was wrong. She became very nervous and ran downstairs to find Jeff.

Once Bonnie told Jeff the news, Jeff immediately grabbed the car keys. Both Jeff and Bonnie went out to search the neighborhood, leaving Connor behind just in case Parker returned. With luck not being in their favor, the sun began going down, and the streetlights were beginning turn on. Bonnie looked at the time on the car dashboard and realized that Parker had been missing for over five hours. Bonnie's nerves became worse, and it resulted in her calling the police.

Jeff and Bonnie went back to their house to meet the police officers. As their conversation unfolded, it seemed as though the police were not taking the incident as seriously as Bonnie would have liked them to. This was because he was not missing for more than twenty-four hours. Because of this, Bonnie became even more stressed than she was prior to calling the police. She began reminiscing about the party and how she should have just pulled Parker aside and talked to him instead of sending everyone home. She continued to blame herself, and what made the situation worse was that she had no idea where she should look to find Parker.

With Connor feeling awful about the entire situation, he thought of one place where Parker might be. With the middle school being close by, Connor ran to the baseball field; and there Parker was, in the dugout, writing in his black book. He ran over to Parker, screaming, "Dude, what the hell are you doing? Mom's going nuts. She has the cops out searching for you!"

He replied, "Yeah, I figured she'd do that. I wanna scare her, Connor . . . She really doesn't understand what we're going through with this move, and now, what makes this all fuckin' worse is that now we have to leave. I looked like a maniac out there today. Who the hell is gonna wanna hang out with me with a temper like that?"

Connor, in agreement, said, "Yeah, bro, what the hell was that about?" Parker seemed just as confused as Connor. He explained, "Truthfully, Connor, I don't know. Ever since I've found out about this move, I've had a type of anger built inside me, and today I was finally able to let some of that out. And it sounds sick, but it felt really good. And I hate saying that, but by writing things down about how I've been feeling and with today actually letting those feelings out, this is the best I've felt in months."

Connor, with a grin on his face, replied, "So you have been writing in your black book?"

"Yeah, man, it's been helping me," said Parker.

"I'm happy it is, man, but we need to get home. Mom's going nuts," Connor suggested.

"All right, but keep all of this between us. Having Mom and Dad thinking I'm crazy is the last thing I need right now," Parker explained.

"You got it, bro. You know I got your back, and thank you for sticking up for me today."

Parker then put his arm around Connor and said, "Of course, man! The only dude that can make fun of you is me! Hahaha! Let's get goin'.'"

Once they got home, Bonnie ran up to both of the boys and gave them a hug. She then looked into Parker's eyes and told him to never do that to them again. With tears building up around Parker's eyelids, he looked at his mom and apologized. With the sheriff walking into the living room, Bonnie told the boys to head upstairs and to start getting ready for bed. Both Bonnie and Jeff needed to finish completing the police paperwork so that if this was to ever happen again, they would have it on file.

Once the police left and they were alone, Jeff went upstairs to check on the boys. He first went to Parker's room, but once again, he was not there. Connor, however, was in the hallway and told his dad that Parker was in the bathroom brushing his teeth. In relief, Jeff said, "Thank God, your mom would have had a heart attack." They both laughed off the moment, but then Jeff pulled Connor into his room to talk to him. "Connor, I just want you to know that I'm very proud of you. Even though things got crazy today, you stayed calm and didn't panic. You brought your brother home in once piece, and that made both your mother and me very happy. I know that you guys both are having a hard time adjusting to this whole move, but it seems like he's having a harder time, so just keep an eye on him, bud."

Connor replied, "I know he is, but I'll keep an eye out on him. He'll be fine."

Jeff then smiled at Connor and said, "All right, big guy, I love you, and tell your brother I love him too."

Before the plans to move came into play, the Shaww family had the perfect life in the perfect little town. With the move unfolding quickly, the Shawws had limited time to mentally adjust to such a big change for them. They would no longer be living in an all-white community with the white picket fence and all the other joys that come with being wealthy in a small town. They'd now be living in the Big Apple, where people never sleep and the lights never turned off. Things are going to be faster, more diverse, and most definitely, more stressful. However, the stress that the Shawws will experience within the first few months in New York City is something they did not expect!

CHAPTER 3

The Big Apple

As they pulled up to the apartment complex they would be living in, the boys instantly knew this was going to be a dramatic change from Brooksville. They went from living in a huge white house with plenty of property and beautiful landscaping to a one-level, three-bedroom condo. Even though, to an ordinary family, this apartment would be a very nice and comfortable living space, the Shawws were not accustomed to living in this type of style. They were used to extravagant things and being the big house on the block. By living in this building, they instantly felt as if they were the same as everyone around them. Now don't get me wrong; the Shawws were very good people and were always respectful toward different classes of people, but they just enjoyed living in a higher-class community. As you can tell, it was going to take some time for them to adjust to this type of lifestyle, but Connor and Parker were hoping that once they made some friends, this entire move would become easier.

The next day came around, and Jeff decided to take the boys around Manhattan. His goal was to teach the boys how the bus and subway systems worked. They were used to either walking to school or getting picked up in their driveway by a yellow school bus. However, now entering high school in Manhattan, they needed to learn how the trains connected and what buses were used to get from point A to point B, which, in their case, was from their apartment complex to their school and vice versa.

As the boys' day came to a close and with the first day of school coming fast, Parker tried to help Connor have more of a cool-kid look. He did this by giving Connor some of his clothes and a baseball cap that always brought Parker good luck. Connor was a bit nervous, as was Parker; however, Parker knew that he would be more outgoing and take more initiative to meet people. This is why he focused more on preparing Connor and making sure that he had the confidence he needed to take on the first day of high school.

The next morning was started by their alarm clocks going off at 6:30 AM. Even though the sound of their clocks did not get them excited to wake up, they each had butterflies in their stomachs that we all once experienced on the first day of high school, not knowing whether or not this was going to be the best or worst day of their lives.

As they both got dressed and prepared to walk out of the house, both Mr. and Mrs. Shaww were waiting by the door with the boys' lunches. Jeff pulled both boys aside before opening the door. "Make sure you guys watch out for each other while you're in school. These kids might be a little different from what you're used to. Just be yourselves and I know you guys will have a great time."

As they left the apartment complex, they made sure to follow the exact route that their dad showed them the previous day. As they hopped on the bus and waited for their stop, Parker could see Connor's knee bouncing up and down. Parker asked Connor if he was okay. "I'm fine, man, just a little nervous, but I'll be all right."

Parker gave Connor a wink and said, "Attaboy."

As their stop was near, they both pressed the yellow button on the side of the windows to notify the bus driver that they needed to get off at the next stop. Once the bus stopped and they took their first step off the bus, they each began walking toward the school. As they got closer, both their stomachs began to tighten up, and the butterflies began to sink in. However, in excitement, Parker looked at Connor and said, "Let's do this!"

Throughout the day, things seemed as if they would be fine; Connor and Parker had three classes together, and one included physical education. This was perfect for Connor because he knew that Parker would stand out among all the other students, which would be a good way for Parker to make friends and then introduce them to him. However, this didn't seem as if it was going to be the case around this neck of the woods.

Both Connor and Parker quickly came to realize that kids in this area were not impressed with athleticism. They both noticed this once they stepped into the gymnasium and no one even changed for gym class. Each boy had on baggy jeans with a long shirt and perfectly white shoes. In similarity, all the girls had on were high-waisted shorts with a belly shirt and, then again, perfectly white shoes.

In Connor's and Parker's eyes, it seemed that all the students in their school wanted was to be friends with kids who were tough and would not take any shit or back down from anyone. With this, they both looked at each other and knew that this was going to take some getting used to.

When they got home after the first day of school, Bonnie and Jeff had dinner made, impatiently waiting for them. During dinner, the boys could tell that their parents were anxious to see how their day went. Bonnie made it quite obvious by staring back and forth between Parker and Connor, and Jeff kept bringing up his day and how welcoming people in his law firm were.

After a few minutes of hearing Jeff speak, Parker began getting worked up, and without hesitation, he stood up and furiously shouted, "Today sucked!" Connor then butted in by saying, "We made no friends, and no one would even look at us. It's literally like a big jungle in there. Everyone does their own thing."

Bonnie, in a calm voice, explained to the boys, "That's a good thing though. What you boys have to understand is that this is high school and the entire freshman class is starting fresh, just like you guys. It's not like Brooksville where you go from the town middle school to the town high school. Kids here get to choose where they want to go to school. So that means they're looking for friends to hang out with just like you two. I'm not saying it's going to be easy, but I promise, if you just put yourself out there, you'll meet people."

Parker bluntly responded, "Okay, Mom."

With that, the next day came around before they knew it, and it was clear that Connor and Parker were not as anxious to wake up from their alarm clock as they were the day before. However, one thing that they both were still very excited about was the idea of being able to find new friends to hang out with.

As they would find out in time, their first six months in the ninth grade had come and gone. Connor and Parker came home every day without having met any new friends, unless they counted their new social studies teacher, Mr. Harris.

Mr. Harris was the one person that both boys had a connection with after the first few weeks of school. He was about fifty-two years old but had the personality of a twenty-year-old. With his upbeat demeanor and blunt honesty, both boys became close to him. Even though they made a connection with someone other than each other, Mr. Harris was not someone they would be able to bring to their house and hang out with.

With Mr. and Mrs. Shaw recognizing the difficulties that the boys were having, it led to the continuation of their fighting. Bonnie felt horrible that they were not fitting in with the new kids in their high school, and what made things worse was that that neither of them could do anything about it.

With the six-month marking period coming to a close, a freshman named José Perez came into the picture. José was a Mexican student who seemed as though he came from a good family with good morals. Parker and Connor kind of got that feeling from José because he seemed different from most of the kids they ran into throughout the year. In simple words, he didn't come off as a hard-ass or wannabe tough guy.

Ironically, Connor and Parker met José in the bathroom during lunchtime. Since Connor and Parker didn't have anyone to hang out with during lunch, they decided to make the bathroom their everyday eating spot. They were able to hang out and talk to each other without feeling as if they were the outsiders in school.

One day, Connor and Parker were both in the bathroom hanging out while eating, and here walked in José with his lunch tray. Immediately, they all looked at one another and gave a small smiling grin. As they introduced themselves and became closer throughout the lunch period and both Connor and Parker were in desperate need of making a friend, they both invited José to join them in the bathroom for lunch for the rest of the school week.

As time went on, they started to hang out outside of school, first by meeting up at the park on the weekends to talk and share stories, and then it led to Mrs. Shaww asking the boys to invite José over for dinner, which Connor and Parker were ecstatic about.

After José met Bonnie and Jeff, the following week, José asked the boys if they wanted to do it again, but this time at his house. After getting permission from their parents, Connor and Parker headed over to José's house on a Friday after school. They all agreed on taking the bus together so that Connor and

Parker would not get lost, since they were still getting used to the MTA (Metropolitan Transportation Authority).

As the day unfolded, Parker and Connor met José's parents and felt they were very nice people. However, one thing that both Connor and Parker realized was that José's dad seemed a little rugged

After meeting them, José pulled Connor and Parker into his room and told them to not be intimidated by his dad. José explained that his dad grew up in a rough neighborhood and had to do some things to make a better life for himself during that time. "He never explained what those things were, but he told me that they still bothered him to this day. That's why he sometimes comes off as a little different. Anyways, now he works in a garage on the corner of Fourth Avenue as a mechanic."

Despite the first impression Connor and Parker got from Santiago, Jose's father, they understood that sometimes people did things that they regretted in life, but just because they had a rough past does not mean that they should be judged strictly on that. This was an easy thing for the boys to forget about, and since then, Connor, Parker, and José became the best of friends. Even though Connor and Parker did not have any other friends other than José, they didn't care because they finally had someone that they could hang out with outside of school.

This, however, was until March 9, when the three of them were in the bathroom eating lunch. Halfway through the period, the school bully, Jimmy Munn, came into the bathroom and started problems. Jimmy Munn and José had an altercation in the past that José actually told Connor and Parker about while they were at the park a few weeks back. José said that Jimmy picked on him all the time because he was Mexican and his dad was a criminal. Connor and Parker never really understood the "criminal" part, but they didn't ask questions because they were genuinely happy to have a friend again.

Jimmy, however, walked into the bathroom like nothing was wrong, walking to the stall as if he was going to mind his own business, but then, he unexpectedly punched José in the stomach. José fell to the ground with the wind knocked out of him; he began huffing and puffing, trying to catch his breath. Jimmy started laughing and began calling him a worthless Mexican—"Just like your father."

With José trying to catch his breath, he stood up as quickly as he could to defend himself; he did this by punching Jimmy back. This was when things began to get ugly, not just for José and Jimmy, but also for Connor and Parker's relationship with José.

With Jimmy being a six-foot-two, two-hundred-pound sophomore, he was effortlessly stronger than five-foot-five, chunky José. Jimmy, in disbelief, grabbed José and threw him into one of the stalls. He then got on top of José while he was in the stall and tightly closed his fist and began beating José in the face.

With Connor and Parker watching, they felt as if they should jump in and help José, but before going to school in New York City, their parents emphasized to them to only get involved in a fight if one of them were in trouble. This led to

Connor screaming for help instead, which, in the end, got Jimmy in trouble.

Ironically, Mr. Harris ran inside the bathroom and began to put Jimmy into a full nelson. Jimmy was no ordinary-sized high school student, so in order to stop the punishment he was putting on José, Mr. Harris had to take necessary action. However, with Jimmy getting pulled off by Larry within a few seconds and Jimmy knowing that Connor was the only one who was screaming for help, it seemed as though Jimmy was pissed at Connor. As Jimmy was being escorted out of the bathroom, Jimmy gazed at Connor with a deep eye stare, which led to Connor thinking. *What if that look meant that he was pissed off at me? Does that mean I'm next?*

Connor didn't know what to think, but one thing he knew was that José was hurt, so he decided to run over to José to help him get up, but unexpectedly, José shrugged off the friendly gesture from Connor and Parker. José was mad, and both Connor and Parker could understand why. He was just embarrassed in front of a lot of students. This was because once Connor screamed out for help, kids in the hallway overheard and ran into the bathroom and began chanting, "Fight, fight, fight!"

After shrugging off Connor and Parker, he began to walk away without talking, but once he got to the end of the hallway, he turned around and looked at Connor and Parker straight in the eyes and said, "I'm not going to have bitches as friends. If you decide to grow a pair within the next three years, find me." This was the first time Connor and Parker heard José speak that way, and the look that José gave to them was not something they were accustomed to seeing from him.

Connor and Parker than stared at each other in disbelief and could not process what had just happened. They knew José was pissed at them and he had a right to be, so instead of chasing after him, they decided to let him blow off some steam, hoping that tomorrow would bring some better luck.

Once they got home, Connor went directly into his room, and Bonnie asked Parker what had happened. Parker explained everything, and Bonnie was proud of Parker for making the smart decision to not get involved, but she knew that losing José as a friend really did affect both of them. Bonnie, Jeff, and Parker felt that it was best to leave Connor alone to allow him to deal with this in his own way.

The next few days went by, and both Parker and Connor overheard people talking about Jimmy and how he was suspended for at least two months. With this being great news for Connor, as the weeks continued to go by without Jimmy in school, the rumors began spreading again. However, this time people were claiming that Jimmy Munn's suspension was ending sooner than expected. Connor knew that he needed to be prepared for Jimmy. As a result, when the weekend came, Connor asked Parker to help him learn how to fight. Parker, being from the same neck of the woods as Connor, really did not have much to teach, but he did say one thing to Connor. "If he does attack you, since he's a lot bigger, I'm not gonna tell you to swing at him, but instead, immediately look around for some type of object that you can pick up and hit him with it, and when you start hitting him, don't stop until he stops."

This was a moment in Connor's life where he knew those words would stick with him forever, and at all costs, he was going to listen to what his brother had to say, even if it did upset his mom and dad.

In regard to Bonnie and Jeff, even though both Connor and Parker were going through a tough time, the boys realized that things between their parents were not the same. Bonnie and Jeff were fighting more often, and Jeff seemed stressed out about his new job. Even though his colleagues were more than welcoming toward him, New York City was filled with a lot more crimes than he was accustomed to, and it led to him being overwhelmed. In Connor's and Parker's eyes, things did not seem as though they were going as planned for any of them.

As the weekend came to a close, Connor knew that Jimmy would be waiting for him, and if he was, Connor was prepared to put into action what Parker had said to him.

With the new week of school taking off, Connor made sure that he was fully aware of who was around him at all times. If things were to get physical between him and Jimmy, he wanted to make sure that Jimmy wasn't going to get a cheap shot in from behind and put Connor at an immediate disadvantage. However, weeks went by, and neither Connor nor Parker had seen Jimmy, and they were curious as to why. The rumor in school was that Jimmy's parents were abusing him and that this time, they really did a number on him, and because of that, he was being homeschooled for the rest of the year. This was music to Connor's ears! Once he heard this, it felt as if a huge cloud was released off his shoulders. Now Connor knew that he wouldn't have to worry about being bullied for the rest of year.

As the second half of the year unfolded, there wasn't much drama in school anymore without Jimmy, but there still was a feeling of emptiness for Connor and Parker because they lost the only friend that they made throughout the past seven months in the city. The one upside that both boys were looking forward to was spring. The reason for that was due to baseball season being in full swing. With that, the boys were beginning to become known around the school. This was due to Parker's baseball skills and Connor being the smart kid. Even though this was definitely an improvement for them, there was still one problem, and that was that they still did not have any real friends. All they did on the weekends was either go to the park to hit the ball around with each other or stay in their apartments and play video games. For such an exciting city, Connor and Parker were having a boring time and didn't understand why it was so hard for them to make friends in the city compared to Brooksville, especially for Parker. They weren't weird, smelly, ugly, or unathletic; I mean, yeah, Connor wasn't the most athletic, but he was still capable of playing sports. Things just weren't getting any easier for them, and they couldn't understand what they were doing wrong, and what made things worse was that they hadn't seen José since the incident in the bathroom and they didn't know what happened to him. It seemed as though everything in this area was just unknown, and they hated it.

With the end of May coming to a close and June taking off, all classes and students were in full throttle. However, some devastating news came about, and that was the rumor that Jimmy Munn returned back to school so that he can finish off the school year and take his regents (New York State exam[s]). Once Connor heard this, he immediately had a psychological breakdown. Connor had a hard time dealing with all the stress of living in the city. He didn't have any friends and wasn't playing any sports, and now he had to go back to worrying about Jimmy. He was nervous that he and Jimmy would get into a fight and Jimmy would embarrass him in front of the entire school, which would make things go from bad to worse. He finally established some type of a rep for himself around school over the past few months, but with Jimmy Munn being back, this would diminish everything he had worked for. Even worse, he would now be known not only as the smart kid but as the weak, smart kid that can't fight.

Connor realized that the only time of day where he felt safe and actually enjoyed himself was when he was in Mr. Harris's class. Mr. Harris, in Connor's eyes, was just a cool dude to hang out with. He was always honest, and Connor loved that. Due to his honesty, Connor felt that speaking to him about his worries might actually help him feel better. This led to Connor pulling Mr. Harris aside after class and asking him to talk; Mr. Harris, of course, agreed. Connor began explaining everything that was going on from the move to losing José and now having to worry about Jimmy Munn again.

Mr. Harris heard everything Connor had to say and understood that this was really affecting Connor. Mr. Harris began by telling Connor to call him Larry, but only when it's just the two of them. He then explained, "In high school, you're gonna go through some tough times, man. Not only are you finding yourself, but also, you're facing people and personalities that you might have never experienced before. You guys are all going through different emotions and hormonal changes at this age, especially these kids that feel that they have to be tough guys to make friends or become known, like Jimmy Munn!

"All I can honestly say to you, Connor, is, if you want to make a name for yourself, just be yourself, buddy. I want you to remember this quote by Bernard Baruch: 'Be who you are and say what you feel, because those who mind don't matter and those who matter don't mind.' You're a great kid that's gonna do great things, but you can't let this move or Jimmy affect you from finding yourself. If he does show up and start problems for you, yes, you might have to stand there and really find yourself in that exact moment, but there's going to be consequences either way. So just be smart with your actions and don't stress about these types of things because they come and go in life, and I'm telling you this from personal experience."

Connor thanked Larry, and it actually made Connor feel a little better. However, in the back of Connor's head, he still knew that Jimmy was coming for him, but he did not know if he would actually do something back if Jimmy was to hit him. Connor kind of assumed that with the time Jimmy had off from being suspended, as well as the time he spent home for homeschooling, Jimmy would have had some time to think about what he did and possibly forgot or forgave Connor for screaming for help. This, however, was just in Connor's imagination.

In just three days of being back in school, Jimmy struck; he beat up a freshman in the school yard for not passing him the basketball during a pickup game. Once Connor heard this, he knew that all his hopes and prayers were not going to be answered.

As another week came and went and school was ending in less than three weeks, Connor almost made it through without crossing paths with Jimmy. On a typical Thursday afternoon, Connor was leaving Mr. Harris's classroom, and as Connor was turning out of the room, he and Jimmy locked eyes. Connor's eyes became still, as if the life was sucked completely out of him. The fire in Jimmy's eyes was like nothing Connor had ever experienced. Jimmy, without hesitation, charged toward Connor with bull-like rage, picking him up and throwing Connor into a locker. The hallway immediately cleared, students pressed up against the lockers, then began cheering.

Connor, stiff as a board, could not get any words out; he was in complete shock. With tears beginning to come out of the corner of his eyes, trying not to show weakness to the kids surrounding him, Connor spotted Parker. At that moment, Connor knew that he was going to be okay. Parker, without hesitation, sneaked up from behind Jimmy and used the three-hundred-page math textbook that he had in his hand and swung it across Jimmy's face, as if he was swinging his bat to hit a baseball. Jimmy instantly collapsed onto the hallway floor, while Parker continued to hit him, repeatedly targeting Jimmy with the book in the back of the head, acting as if Parker was once again releasing some type of emotion and built-up anger.

The surrounding kids started cheering Parker's name, and just then, like a vision in a movie, Connor had a flashback to when the fight broke for their going-away party. However, this time felt different; it was no longer the "uh-oh" feeling he experienced in his backyard, but this time, the feeling was if things were about to change for the better!

After Jimmy stopped moving, Parker finally stopped his brutal punishment. He then looked around and saw everyone standing around, cheering his name. Connor looked at him with excitement, but all Parker did was grab Connor and run toward the south-end staircase. Connor, still filled with excitement, was brought back to reality by Parker pulling on his shirt to get up. Parker was not happy with himself, and even though it made him feel that exhilarating feeling once again, he looked directly into Connor's eyes and emphasized, "You will never do that, unless it has to be done."

Once both boys got home, Parker went straight for his room. Connor, still filled with adrenaline, decided to start throwing punches in midair, as if he was Rocky Balboa or someone. Bonnie walked into the room and asked Connor why he was doing this. Connor then explained in full detail what happened at school, not thinking that it would be a problem because Parker was defending him. However, after hearing what Connor said, Jeff and Bonnie called Parker down to talk to him, asking Connor to go to his room. Connor left but did not go far. He stood behind the kitchen wall and listened to the conversation that they were having. The first thing that both parents said was that they were proud of Parker for defending Connor; however, they were upset that he continued to beat on Jimmy once he hit the floor.

Prior to the fight in school, Bonnie and Jeff both felt that things have been weird with Parker lately, and they figured it was just him adjusting to the new city. They wanted to figure out a way for Parker to release some stress without actually putting it into aggression. With that, they decided to pull out another black book. They told Parker that this could be his "safe book." In a loving, charismatic, and motherly tone, Bonnie explained,

"Whatever you decide to write in here, it will be yours and no one else's. Write your thoughts, emotions, and questions." The problem with this was that they gave Parker this book without knowing that he was already using the black book that Connor gave him for Christmas as a type of "comfort journal."

Parker thanked Bonnie and Jeff so that he can get back up to his room, but on the way back to his room, Parker decided to put the book onto his computer desk, it didn't seem as if he had much interest in it because he already had the journal Connor gave him, and so far, it was doing the job, or so Connor thought.

Parker has always been the strong one in the family. He never liked to talk about his feelings; he figured that if he left them alone, they would eventually go away. In contrast, Connor was the complete opposite. He loved the thought of writing feelings down into a journal and being able to keep notes of everything he was feeling on a specific day. It was an idea that subconsciously, Connor knew he would take part in.

With Parker keeping to himself for the rest of the day and Connor doing the same, the night went by fast, and the next day was upon them. Parker was hesitant to go back to school because he didn't want anyone bringing up the fight; he was over it and wanted the whole situation to be done with.

Meanwhile, as the boys approached their school, they both sensed that something was different, similar to the feeling Connor was experiencing after the fight. As they walked in the school, both boys noticed that people were staring, people that neither Connor nor Parker ever spoke to or saw before.

Unexpectedly, a freshman within the hallways smiled and waved to them, especially Parker; these actions continued throughout the entire day, as if people now had some type of respect for the boys. The rest of the week ended up being the best week of Parker's school year—not only because of the fight, but because people were beginning to respect him, just like they once were in Brooksville. This led to Parker beginning to meet new people.

The good luck did not stop there for Parker. Parker, as the school week came to an end, realized that the upcoming weekend was the New York Yankee game that Jeff surprised Parker with for Christmas. The timing couldn't have been better for Jeff and Parker. This was because Parker could now tell people that he was going to the Yankees game, and for Jeff, he felt that it would bring him and Parker closer again, just like old times. Jeff realized that the past few months have been tough for all of them and they haven't been able to do much together to take their minds off things and this game would be a way for them to start fresh.

With Saturday coming around and game day finally among them, Parker could not have been any more excited! This game was the first thing that Parker was excited about since living in New York City, and Jeff knew that if things went well, it would put some light on the move. Parker's anticipation of experiencing his first Yankees game had him going crazy. He could not wait until he finally stepped through the gates and smelled the wet dew from the fresh-cut grass. That was Parker's favorite part of playing baseball.

As they entered the stadium and sat down in their seats, Parker made sure to take in the moment and to really enjoy himself with his dad. As the game unfolded and the Yankees took the lead in a dramatic finish at home plate in the bottom of the ninth, the night couldn't have ended any better. However, Jeff had other plans! As they left the stadium, Jeff asked one of Yankee fans where the closest ice cream shop was relative to the stadium. The spectator explained where they could find one, pointing them in the right direction, and Jeff and Parker began their walk.

On their way to the Carvel ice cream shop, Jeff needed to stop at an ATM to take out money. With Parker in the back of his father while Jeff was taking out cash, a man dressed in all-black clothing unexpectedly held up both Parker and Jeff. Neither Jeff nor Parker was able to see the man's face because he had a mask on that covered up to his nose. Jeff knew that something was off and this was no ordinary man; this was a robbery.

Immediately, Jeff tried to hand over the money that he had in his pockets, but with him trembling due to his nerves, it looked as if he was reaching for something in his pocket. The robber, not taking any chances, pulled out a nine-millimeter pistol and shot over the top of Jeff's head, causing Jeff to fall to the cement. With Jeff being dazed but not fully unconscious, he looked up and desperately asked the robber what he wanted. The robber pointed at Parker using his gun. Without hesitation, Jeff lunged for the robber's leg and began pulling him down to the ground, trying to distract him so that Parker could get away. Parker, in shock, did not know what to do. Continuously, Jeff screamed to Parker throughout the tussle to run, but Parker was frozen solid.

Once Jeff got the robber down to the ground, he took the upper hand. He was then able to get on top of the robber while attempting to choke him so that he would pass out. However, without Jeff realizing, the robber reached for his waist and pulled out a sharp knife from under his shirt and penetrated Jeff's stomach. Jeff instantly became as stiff as a board and rolled off the robber. Parker became aware of what had just happened and snapped out of his shocked state and took off into the opposite direction. With the black-clothed robber on the ground, he noticed Parker was getting way, which led to him reaching for his gun and firing it toward Parker. After the third bullet was shot, Parker then hit the ground, with a bullet penetrating the side of his head.

Later on that night, the telephone woke up Bonnie at 11:30 PM; she received the news. Immediately, without waking Connor, she raced her way to the hospital. The news was heartbreaking; Jeff died due to the puncture wound causing a large amount of blood to be lost. As for Parker, he was in critical condition, fighting his way through surgery.

With his surgery being finished, the doctors told Bonnie that they were able to stop the blood that was causing his brain to lose oxygen. However, due to having a lack of oxygen going to his brain for such a long amount of time, the doctors explained it could potentially result in him having permanent brain damage.

With an hour passing, the doctors once again approached Bonnie with more devastating news. They informed Bonnie that Parker had fallen into a coma. Things went from bad to worse, and for the Shaww family, it seemed as though things were beginning to collapse.

Bonnie, however, was now a widow, and her other son had a slim chance of surviving. With this type of situation being tough to handle for anyone, Bonnie had to figure out a way to tell her other fourteen-year-old son about his father and brother. She repeatedly asked herself, "Should I tell him that Parker is alive or dead?" She knew that either way, this would destroy him, but she also understood that if she told Connor that both of them were gone, he would have to begin the healing process and would not have to hang on and hope for Parker to recover. She understood that the chances of Parker snapping out of his coma were slim to none, due to the amount of blood loss and lack of oxygen to his brain. In her opinion, she felt that it would be best to tell Connor that both Dad and Parker were gone. And when she went home earlier that morning that is exactly what she told him.

In that exact moment, Connor did not know what to say or do. He was caught off guard and did know what was going on. All he asked was "How?" After Bonnie told him, he didn't know whether or not to cry or be angry. He asked if they were going to have a funeral for them. With Bonnie not telling Connor the truth regarding to Parker, she told Connor, "We're going to have them both cremated so that we can have them with us at all times." Connor couldn't believe that any of this was happening, and was in complete shock.

As the day went on, Connor could not stop crying, pacing back and forth between Parker's room and his parents' room, feeling more helpless than ever. Eventually Connor would lay down on his parents' bed and fall asleep next to his mom. He woke up later that day and wanted to believe that last night was just a terrible nightmare, but after seeing paperwork his mom brought home from the hospital, he knew that last night really happened and his dad and brother were gone forever.

Later on that day, with Connor's curiosity and depressed state kicking in, he did not want to believe what his mother had told him. With him being the person and student that he is, he needed some type of visual clarification that this truly happened. As a result, he headed for the hospital where both Jeff and Parker were brought the night before. On the train ride to the hospital, Connor could not stop but think, *Who would want to kill them?* Everything was just getting worse and worse, and Connor knew that if his dad and especially Parker were really gone, he could not go on much longer. Connor felt as if he hit rock bottom.

After he got off the train, he walked an additional two blocks to reach the hospital. As he approached the front of the hospital, out of nowhere, Connor was getting stomach pains, but he was determined to see his dad and brother one last time. Walking into the hospital as if it were a life-and-death situation, Connor was as pale as a ghost; with cold sweat coming down the top of his forehead, he walked up to the receptionist at the hospital and asked where he could find the identification room so that he would be able to identify his brother's and father's bodies. The women at the desk answered him and pointed him in the right direction. Connor slowly walked toward the elevator, but for some reason, one thing that the receptionist said to him made him think that maybe there was some type of miracle that Parker was still alive. She told him that he had to go to the second floor, which ironically was Parker's baseball number, like his favorite player, Derek Jeter on the Yankees. Connor felt that this was some type of sign from God and that there was no way that Parker was dead.

As the elevator stopped, Connor slowly walked off. As a doctor greeted him, the doctor respectively asked Connor to follow him. As he timidly approached the morgue sign, he was then brought into a cold room surrounded by blue-and-white wall tiles with white marble floors. This is where Connor saw what he thought was his father's body laying on a silver table, with a bright light reflecting off of a white bed sheet. Walking into the room gave Connor the chills. It was extremely cold and quiet. He knew the body underneath the sheet was his dad, and it began to make him sick. As Connor and the doctor approached the body, the doctor asked Connor if he was ready. Connor nodded, and the doctor folded over the sheet and allowed Connor to see his father for one last time. Once Connor saw his dad lying there with a ghostlike complexion, he immediately collapsed; he couldn't believe he was really gone. The pain in Connor's gut intensified, and the feeling of living without his dad or brother was horrifying.

Even though losing his father was tough for Connor to deal with, he knew this experience would not be the worse feeling he would feel today. This resulted in him pulling himself together and asking to see his brother, and the doctor replied, "Follow me." Connor was confused and asked why he wasn't in the same room as his dad, and the doctor answered respectively with "Parker is in ICU. I will take you there now." The pain in Connor's stomach went from feeling as if knives were penetrating his stomach to unexpectedly having butterflies take over his body. At that exact moment, Connor didn't know what to think. He knew that Parker couldn't have been dead; "He was superman."

Superman, however, was never hurt the way Parker was, and Connor realized that when he spotted Parker through the room's glass doors. He could see that Parker was severely hurt, with tubes and needles coming in and out of his body and a large white bandage covering the entire right side of his face.

Even though all these unfortunate occurrences would make an ordinary person lose faith, Connor still felt that there was some type of hope that Parker would somehow pull through. This, however, was until he saw the trachea pushing air in and out of Parker's lungs. Parker was no longer breathing on his own. Connor never saw his brother this way—so powerless and nonresponsive. This perception of Parker was something Connor was not accustomed to seeing, and he didn't want to believe this was really his big brother. It caused Connor to have his first panic attack. He could not get the mental image out of his head of his brother dying. This caused Connor to take off without saying a word to the doctor and headed straight for the train station.

As Connor stood on the train platform, with the noise of the train getting closer and the unknown voices behind him filling his mind with confusion, Connor slowly crept up to the edge of the platform and began contemplating what he was about to do He thought, "Maybe if I jump onto the tracks and get hit by a train, I could die. And if I die, I'd eventually be with Parker. It's just a matter of time until he's dead too, so why not?" With this idea going through his head and the train getting closer, Connor saw Parker's face, and he knew that Parker would be disappointed with him. "Parker wouldn't want this for me. Parker would want me to stay strong and have faith that he was going to pull through." With that, Connor tried to change his mind-set within those last few seconds and to do his best to think more optimistically about his father's death and brother's critical condition.

With the ten-minute train ride being over, Connor walked back to the condo. Once Connor walked inside his house, he went directly into Parker's room. It was the first time Connor ever went into Parker's room and felt alone. After walking around the room and looking through Parker's things, Connor decided to lie on Parker's bed and fell into a deep sleep.

CHAPTER 4

Parker?

With the school year being over and summer beginning, this was going to be Connor's first summer without Parker. Even though Connor was discouraged and extremely upset about this, he promised himself that he would keep himself busy.

Since the summer started, one thing that Connor would do every day thus far was consistently swing Parker's baseball bat in the backyard. As the first few weeks of summer went by, Connor was beginning to get impatient. He wanted to know who killed his father and injured Parker, but neither he nor his mother had heard anything back from the police. This led to Parker beginning to visit the police station on a weekly basis. The cops, however, would not give Connor much information; all they continuously said was "We'll keep you updated on any information we find out." Continuously hearing this was beginning to get under Connor's skin. He didn't understand why this murder was not the cops' number one priority.

✓ Connor

Meanwhile, one night, while Connor was sleeping, Bonnie came home from work and was stunned with what she found in the kitchen. She immediately ran into Connor's room, waking him up from his sleep. She began screaming at him and repeatedly asked, "Connor, what did you do?"

Connor, being half asleep, answered, "Mom, I didn't do anything. Ask Parker." After hearing Connor's response, Bonnie Immediately stood still and closed the door. It all clicked for Bonnie. She knew that Connor was still extremely upset and, because of that, it seemed as though he decided to act out in a way that would get Bonnie's attention. With Connor answering the way that he did, Bonnie let the issue go and continued on with her night.

With Bonnie teaching during the school year, things were tough financially, but they managed to get by. However, with summer now in full effect and there being no husband to help with the bills, she had to find another job. This led to her finding a waitressing position at an Italian restaurant. The pay was not great, so this led to her having to work doubles and, sometimes, the graveyard shift to take care of the late-night, early-morning workers. At this point, she would do anything to take care of herself and Connor, but by the time she got home, she was always exhausted.

Within a few weeks, Bonnie went from a well-taken-cared-of wife to a widow fighting to keep food on the table for her one son while her other son was fighting for his life in the hospital.

As the night came to a close and the next day began, Connor went through his typical summer day routine. Once again, he found himself sitting at the police station, waiting for some type of information on his dad's case. A police officer named Kenny Smith, a man Connor grew to have a relationship with over the past few weeks, told Connor that he could sit at his desk throughout the day since he was going to be out in the street.

Kenny, in Connor's eyes, seemed like a good guy and acted as if he truly wanted to help Connor find the person who killed his father. Connor, however, knew this opportunity might not come around again, so being the computer wiz that he is, Connor knew he could take advantage of being at Kenny's desk. Using his computer skills and his memory, Connor was able to put Officer Smith's badge number into his log-in screen, and there it was, full access to the entire police database. It seemed as though Connor was not, by any means, the innocent little freshman he was just a few months prior. By hacking into the database, Connor was able to access his father's files. After doing a few minutes of research, he noticed a blue video link connected to the case file. Quickly, Connor realized that the video link was of his dad's murder. He didn't understand how that was even possible, but then Connor remembered that his mom told him that his father was killed in front of an ATM, and it seemed as though the video was taken through the ATM video recording.

After clicking on the link and witnessing his dad being murdered for the first time, Connor remained still for a few moments. Even though the pit in his stomach was sickening, Connor knew that he had to go more in-depth with his research. He was able to use the computer's technical resources to zoom in and out on the robber's face. Even though the robber had a mask on that was covering his forehead, nose, and mouth, a large chunk of his eyes and eyebrows was showing. Even with the limited amount of space that was showing, Connor knew that he had recognized the murderer's face but didn't understand how.

Immediately after putting together what he just saw, Connor went back to the condo. He began to drive himself crazy trying to figure out where he recognized that face. He began to lose his temper, swinging Parker's bat around the house and breaking lamps as well as his bed frame. Connor had no one to talk to about the problems he was going through, and that was the issue Connor had the most problem dealing with. He always had Parker to release his thoughts onto, but now, there was no one!

As the summer days continued to go by, days became weeks, and before Connor knew it, he realized that he spent over two months of his summer trying to put the eyes and eyebrows to an actual face. The frustration had eventually gotten to Connor, and so he decided that he needed to call it quits, at least for now.

The mental toll that this summer took on Connor was unbelievable. This was something that was on his mind 24-7 throughout the entire summer, and it caused him to be extremely frustrated and angry toward himself and others. The only good thing about the summer was that the doctors told Connor that Parker seemed as if he was beginning to become more responsive to the treatment they were giving him. With the doctors telling Connor this, it gave him some hope.

With school starting up again in less than a week, Connor decided to try to prepare himself for the tenth grade without his best friend on his side. He began thinking about ninth grade and how the situation with Jimmy Munn unfolded. Connor truthfully felt that over the past few months, he had been through so much up to this point that he didn't feel that Jimmy would be able to hurt him any worse than he already had been. It was something that Connor knew was inevitable, and this would be the first challenge he would have to face without Parker.

With school beginning and the first month flying by and Jimmy Munn still partaking in his old habits, Connor was trying not to worry too much about him. All he wanted was to see Parker in school again and to graduate as quickly as possible with his best friend on his side.

With Connor going to the hospital every day after school without Bonnie knowing, he would go and talk to Parker. He would talk to Parker as if he was fully functioning. Every time Connor talked to him, he would hold his hand.

With it being four months since the incident, even though the doctor said he was responding better to the treatment, Parker was beginning to lose a lot of muscle mass, which was changing his appearance. However, one day at the hospital, while Connor was talking to Parker, Parker squeezed Connor's hand; Connor didn't know what that meant, and so he screamed for the doctors. As the head doctor came running in, asking what was wrong, Connor told Dr. Chung what had happened. After Dr. Chung caught his breath and took in what Connor had said, he sat down next to Connor and spoke with him. He explained, "Sometimes in these types of comas, the brain is still functioning, which leads to muscle spasms, and that's all Parker was probably doing when he squeezed your hand, Connor. I'm really sorry to disappoint you."

Connor, in disbelief, did not agree with Dr. Chung. "You said 'probably,' so there's still a possibility that he heard me, correct? I've been here for months, and he's never done that, so I know he's going to be coming out of this soon. Just watch."

Dr. Chung put his hand on Connor's shoulder with a smile on his face and said, "I hope so, Connor."

Connor's patience had begun to grow short, and his brain was taking a huge punishment for the stress that he was under. After leaving the hospital in extreme hostility, Connor went directly home and found his way into Parker's room. With Parker's room being the only place where he felt safe, he sat on Parker's bed once again and fell asleep.

The next morning, Connor was woken by the sunlight peeking through the blinds of Parker's bedroom window as well as two familiar voices coming from the kitchen. As Connor got out of bed and began to walk out of the room, following the sound of the voices, he was surprised to see his mother and Mr. Harris talking to each other in the kitchen. Connor was completely stumped! He didn't understand why Mr. Harris was in his house.

After taking notice of Connor, Mr. Harris stood up and shook Connor's hand and asked how he was doing. Connor, still in shock, not saying a word, was then saved by Bonnie. "Mr.

Harris and I ran into each other the other day when he came into the restaurant for lunch. I guess we look alike, Connor, because he instantly asked if I was your mother. After that, I began talking to him, and he was telling me about the things that were going on in school."

Mr. Harris then jumped in, "Yeah, buddy, I don't really hear from you anymore now that you're a sophomore. You know you could always come in and hang out, right?" Connor didn't really know what to say about the entire situation, but he told Mr. Harris that he appreciated the offer and that he might take him up on it.

As the day went on, Mr. Harris was still over at the Shawws' apartment and was invited by Bonnie to stay for dinner. Even though it was only a few months after Jeff died, Connor noticed that this was the first time since his father's death that his mom was smiling and laughing again. Connor was still a little suspicious of Mr. Harris's intentions, but by seeing Bonnie enjoying herself, Connor tried not to stress about the entire situation too much.

With the night coming to a close and dinner being over, Mr. Harris knocked on Connor's door and walked in.

"Hey, Connor, just wanted to say thank you for allowing me to stay for dinner. I know the last few months have been hard for you, and I don't want me hanging around your mom to make your healing process any more difficult for you. So if anything bothers you, just tell me."

"You're fine, Larry. It was good to see my mom smiling again."

Connor was not very talkative toward Mr. Harris because he wasn't sure exactly how he felt about the entire situation yet. All he wanted was for his mom to be happy, and if it was Mr. Harris that did that for her, so be it.

Once Mr. Harris left, Connor went into the living room to talk with his mother. "So what's the deal with Larry?"

Bonnie looked at Connor with a grin. "Honestly, Connor, we were talking about you the entire time. He was telling me about the conversations you had last year when Jimmy was bothering you. It seems like Mr. Harris really likes you. You should go into his classroom sometime and talk with him. Maybe you can open up to him a little bit since you don't really talk to me about how you are doing."

"I don't know, Mom. Don't you find it kind of weird that he 'ironically' had lunch at your restaurant and found his way back to our apartment to talk about just me?"

Bonnie, in confusion, suspiciously asked, "What are you saying, Connor? You think he's up to something? From what he told me, I thought you guys seemed pretty close."

Connor explained, "We were close, and he's a good guy. I just don't know. Maybe I'm just overthinking everything. I'll try to stop by his room and talk to him a little bit."

With the night coming to an end and the morning sun waking Connor up once again, he began to get ready for school. As Connor walked his way to the bus station, he remembered that he had gym class later that day. However, even though Connor usually loved gym class, because it allowed him to be physically active, he realized that the next sport being played was baseball. This was a sensitive subject for Connor. Any type of baseball involvement made him think of Parker, which made him sad, especially since he hasn't had much time lately to visit Parker in the hospital.

The whole day was sort of a ticking time bomb for Connor. He knew each period was getting closer and closer to gym class. As he walked into the gymnasium, he realized that everyone was headed outside to put the class into action.

As the class unfolded, even though it was a difficult time for Connor, the class was going well, and everyone was enjoying themselves. Connor was trying to think more optimistically about being out in the field again because he knew Parker would be ecstatic if he was out there playing the sport that he loved. By coming to terms with this, it allowed Connor to enjoy himself a little more than he expected to.

As the score tallied up and the final inning came to an end, everyone began walking off the field. Meanwhile, Jimmy Munn, out of nowhere, decided to throw a baseball at Connor's head. Connor, without being fully conscious, hit the dirt. As he tried to get up to his knees, he realized that he was extremely dazed and didn't know what was going on. However, he was able to make out some of his vision as he began to come to. With the small amount of space that he was able to clearly make out, Connor thought he saw Parker. He didn't know whether he was still really messed up or it really was him. All he thought was, *How is it possible?*

In and out of his dazed state, all Connor could think was, *Is it really him? Is this a surprise? Is he back?* Even though it seemed as though Parker was physically back to normal, there was something different in the eyes of Parker; he seemed mad! Within ten seconds, Parker was on top of Jimmy, beating him with a baseball bat. Parker did not stop until there was blood coming out the side of Jimmy's face. Everyone began chanting, and when he heard that noise, Connor knew he was back.

Connor asked himself, *Are they cheering because Parker is back and they're happy for me?"* Connor, in that moment, did not know what to think, but he didn't care;, Parker was back!

As happy as he could be, Connor felt like he and Parker were back to being a unit again. As the chanting stopped, Connor ran over to Parker and asked him how this was possible. In excitement, Parker explained, "Dude, the doctors literally said it was a miracle. But listen, I can't stay for long. The docs don't know that I'm here. I've been in physical therapy for the past few weeks, and they don't know that I sneaked out."

Connor jumped in, cutting Parker off, "You've been out for a few weeks, and we haven't gotten a phone call or anything?"

Parker then explained, "I guess the doctor said that he tried calling you guys but no one answered the phone, and there was no answer machine to leave a message."

Connor, still in shock but in agreement, told Parker, "That makes sense. I'm either at school or trying to figure out who did this to you and Dad, and Mom's been working like a maniac. But, dude, it's really good to see you!"

Parker, impatiently trying to get out of there, cut Connor off, "How is Dad?" Connor, immediately getting a saddened look on his face, had to break the news to Parker. Parker's new sense of rejuvenation and second chances instantly faded into the black bottomless pit that Connor was experiencing over the past few months.

Connor then grabbed Parker. "Don't worry, I'm gonna make the person who did this to Dad and you pay for what he did. I promise."

Parker still couldn't believe what he heard but left off with Connor by saying, "I have to go, but do me a favor and don't tell anyone that I showed up, because I could get in a lot of trouble, and do yourself a favor—stay away from the hospital. Let me work on getting fully recovered, and you keep working on finding who did this to me and Dad." DAD & ME

"Of course," said Connor.

As Parker left and Connor walked back into the building, a teacher ran over to him and dragged Connor into the principal's office. Connor, under the impression that they didn't see Parker, was happy because then Parker wouldn't get in trouble. As a result, Connor took the blame without question and was agreeing to everything that the principal was saying to him. The principal let Connor off with only a two-week suspension. Connor believed that the principal had some type of sympathy for him because of the loss of his father at the end of last school year.

Connor was initially happy to be suspended, but then he realized that Parker would be at the hospital, not at home. After coming home from school that day, Connor lay down in Parker's bed. He hadn't been able to sleep in his own bed since the incident. Fortunately, Connor didn't have to give his mom an explanation for Parker beating the crap out of Jimmy; this was because Connor barely saw his mom anymore due to her having to work two jobs because of Jeff not being there anymore to help support them. The only time Bonnie really has time to relax is between 12:00 AM and 6:00 AM, and that's right before Connor usually wakes up for school.

Meanwhile, once Connor got into Parker's bed and began looking around him, he realized that he moved some things around Parker's room over the past couple of months. This resulted in Connor trying to reorganize Parker's stuff so that he wasn't mad at Connor for changing things around.

In addition, while Connor was moving things back to normal, he discovered the black journal that he gave to Parker the week of Christmas over a year and a half ago.

Connor felt as if he hadn't seen the journal since the day Parker threw it in the corner of the room when he was upset. Connor thought, *How is that even possible though? Had I been walking past this book every day and not recognized it on the side of Parker's bed? Or maybe . . . Parker was already home and made it noticeable for me to see. Who knows.*

As Connor reached down for the journal and flipped through the first few pages, he realized that half the journal was full. He didn't understand how that was possible. Connor only saw Parker write in it a handful of times, but Connor thought, *I guess he really did like the whole journal idea.* Even though Connor still did not understand how this was all possible, with his excitement of Parker being back, Connor tried not to overthink about it too much.

However, the ironic factor about Parker's writing was that, for Connor, he understood the emotion and pain Parker was dealing with during the time he was writing because Connor was experiencing a similar feeling before Parker showed up at the baseball field and throughout the entire summer.

As Connor continued to read, he realized that Parker had a lot of issues that he never talked to Connor about. Even though these issues were similar to his own, Connor realized that Parker's feelings might be a little more severe. He wrote about hitting things and killing animals. Connor couldn't believe what he was reading. *Killing animals?* Connor thought, *Why would he be killing things, and how could he physically kill something, especially something so innocent as an animal?* These were questions that Connor wanted to ask Parker for himself, but he hadn't seen him since the school incident earlier in the day.

The most intriguing story in the book that Connor took notice of was about ten pages, and it involved Parker killing a stray cat. This was a neighborhood cat that Connor saw a handful of times since they lived in the city and was curious as to why he never saw it anymore. Parker, however, cleared this up throughout a few pages.

Throughout those couple of pages, Parker emphasized on the feeling that it gave him and how he loved it. "The feeling of power. The feeling of being in control of someone's or something's life. It was my first time, and I knew it definitely wasn't going to be my last." Parker wrote, "I killed the cat in the best way possible . . . the microwave. I stuffed the black cat on the microwave dish and closed the microwave door. I set the timer to one minute! The anticipation I felt was like no other."

As Connor continued reading this, he began putting the puzzle pieces together. Connor knew exactly what Parker was feeling. Connor related it to the feeling he got when he witnessed Parker beating up Jimmy Munn for the first time.

As Connor continued reading, Parker then wrote, "As the dish began spinning and the timed minute turned into seconds, I began hearing the cat making funny noises, like a more defined purr. Then, out of nowhere, I saw the cat beginning to warp, such as a water bottle when you light the plastic on fire. It was an image I never saw in my life. The cat's stomach began to expand, and the cat's eyes became extremely glossy. Within twenty-five seconds, the black-furred cat turned into a red dress, and when the microwave finally beeped, it was completely disfigured."

While reading the last few words, Connor stopped and had a déjà vu experience. He suddenly thought back to a few weeks prior, when Bonnie walked into his room in the middle of the night yelling at him. *Maybe that's why Mom was freaking out that night*, Connor thought, and he was curious to know if Parker came around prior to today.

Reading Parker's journal was not something Connor should be doing, and he knew that, but he was glad that he did. He realized that he and Parker were going through some similar feelings, and maybe with Parker being back, they would be able to talk about a few things, particularly his journal.

CHAPTER 5

Life with Parker

After the suspension was over, Connor went back to school. Things, however, seemed a little different. People were looking at Connor as if they feared him. He figured that Parker was beginning to be the protective brother that Connor knew him as and told people to stay away from him before he left, or simply enough, they were afraid of Parker after what they saw what he did to Jimmy. With Connor putting two and two together, he went on with his day. This didn't really bother Connor because he truly missed Parker and the way things used to be. However, one thing that was bothering Connor lately was the fact that he was beginning to think about José a lot. He hadn't seen him in a while and didn't understand why. Rumor had it that he was now in what kids called special classes. Connor was confused when he heard this. He knew José was a smart kid and didn't think he had any type of learning disability.

With Connor being who he was, he did some research of his own. He pulled the same stunt that he did in the police station and decided to utilize his relationship with Mr. Harris.

At the end of the day, he walked into Mr. Harris's office and asked him if he would mind if he stayed in his room to do some homework. Connor figured he would just wait until Mr. Harris left or went to the bathroom so he could hack into Larry's school account. Luckily, Mr. Harris told Connor, "I'm actually getting out of here. I have a hot date, but I'll leave the door open for you. All you have to do is close it when you're leaving." Connor played the part and agreed with Mr. Harris's terms, not asking any questions.

With this, Connor's plan couldn't have gone any more smoothly. He was able to access José's school transcript, and one of the first things that Connor noticed was the words *depression disorder* highlighted in yellow.

Connor didn't understand why José was depressed out of nowhere. The only thing Connor could think of was, maybe he was depressed about the incident with Jimmy Munn and with him and Parker not doing anything to help him. It also could have been that he didn't have any friends since he dropped Connor and Parker. The whole situation really messed with Connor, and at the same time, it truly made Connor feel bad about the entire Jimmy Munn incident last year.

As a few days passed and this became an issue that Connor wanted to fix, he decided to make it a priority to find José in school and work things out. Friday came, and Connor was determined to find José. Extremely uncharacteristic of Connor, he decided to skip ninth period to get an early jump on José before he headed for the bus.

After searching for half the school period, Connor finally found the room that he was looking for. As he crept up toward the window of the classroom door, he spotted José, and all of a sudden, Connor went into shock. After seeing José's face, he knew who killed his dad. Connor couldn't believe it. He didn't know whether to be happy or angry, frustrated, or relieved; it was a feeling that Connor was not familiar with—the feeling of vengeance but, at the same time, confusion. Connor began pacing back and forth, asking himself, *How is that possible? Why would he do that? What did I ever do to him?* Connor couldn't believe it. However, all he did know was that he needed to tell Parker.

Connor began walking away but heard someone behind him. He then turned around and spotted Parker and brought him into the bathroom. Connor first asked Parker what he was doing here. Parker explained, "I told you, I sneak out. I only have limited time, and I knew you'd be in school, so I wanted to see you before having to go back." Connor smiled but then anxiously began telling Parker everything.

After hearing what Connor had to say, Parker felt that it made sense and told Connor that he agreed with him about taking action and getting some revenge. Connor then told Parker to slow down.

"Listen, man, I know this might be out of my place, but I read your journal, and if you're talking about revenge in the way of killing, I don't know if I can do that." Despite Connor reading

Parker's journal without permission, Parker completely directed his attention toward revenge. He emphasized to Connor, "This guy killed our father—killed Dad! We have to do something." With that, Connor agreed, and it led to the boys coming up with a plan, a plan to catch their father's murderer and make him suffer the way Connor, Parker, and Bonnie have been suffering over the past few months.

They wanted payback, and with that, they decided to make an agreement with each other and become a team—a team with the goal of finding their dad's killer and making them pay for what they did and finally giving their father's death some justice and putting Bonnie at ease.

After talking, Connor and Parker knew that they each felt the exact same way about this entire situation, but Connor, being the more realistic and intelligent brother, knew that this goal would not be accomplished without a plan being put into action, some direction, and organization.

After reading Parker's journal, Connor knew they had to start off with little things, which consisted of hurting or killing other people or animals so that they would be prepared once their moment came. Parker was sloppy, and Connor knew that by the cat incident. With that, they agreed on practicing with animals and then eventually moving toward killing people in the near future; this was so when the opportunity came for them to kill their father's murderer, there would not be any type of hesitation.

An additional agreement that they had was that they would not kill ordinary people. The people they would target would have to have zero purpose in this world, people like homeless individuals, people with no future and who live on the streets. They figured this wouldn't be too big of an issue, due to them living in New York City and hobos being killed in back alleys on an everyday basis, either by overdosing or by being stabbed by another drug addict who wanted drugs. They agreed to talk more, but Parker had limited time. Connor agreed to walk back to the hospital with Parker so that they could discuss the plan.

As they began walking, Connor had to get something off his chest to Parker. He explained that he wasn't going to be able to kill someone. "I honestly don't feel that I could take the life out of someone. Just the thought of piercing someone in the heart with a knife and having their heartbeat slow down until it comes to a complete stop gives me the creeps." With Parker hearing this, they both agreed that Connor would be the brain of the operation, meaning that Connor would come up with the ideas of who exactly they were going to hurt or kill and how and where it would be done.

One thing that Connor did want done, however, was for Parker to continue writing inside of his journal, explaining in detail what happens during these planned attacks. Connor wanted this because, even though he couldn't kill someone, he knew that by reading it through the words of Parker, he would be able to experience some type of vision and fulfillment. Connor wanted some type of satisfaction, and he truly felt that he would receive this through the words of his brother. He also felt that by Parker writing things down, it might somehow make him feel a little better.

As they came to an agreement and they got closer to the hospital, Connor and Parker split ways. As the day continued, Connor eventually got to his apartment, did some homework, and passed out.

Saturday morning came, and once again, he was awoken by laughs. He stood up and walked into the living room, and there Mr. Harris and Bonnie were, with Bonnie's feet crossed over on Larry's legs. It seemed as though Mr. Harris was in sleeping clothes, as if he slept over. They both quickly stood up and said hi to Connor. Connor was a little confused and asked what Larry was doing there. Bonnie began speaking, but then Larry cut in and asked if it was okay to tell him; Bonnie approved and Larry began explaining.

"All right, so I know this is a little weird, seeing your old schoolteacher in your house in the morning, but remember when I told you yesterday that I had a hot date?" Connor nodded. "Well, that was your mother. I know this is tough to swallow, and that's why I'm explaining it to you. This isn't your mom's doing. I asked her to join me for dinner, and she agreed. But if this bothers you, I know you've both been through a lot over the past year, and I don't want to cause any more stress for either of you. Just let me know what you want, Connor, and either way, your mother and I will understand."

Connor, without much emotion being shown, simply said, "I'm fine with it, Larry. Just treat her good." Of course, Larry responded. Connor walked into his bedroom and began talking to himself, "I can't believe this shit. It hasn't even been a year yet . . . Is she serious? I know she's lonely, but damn . . . And my teacher! I want her happy, but Larry? I gotta tell Parker."

As Connor began to calm down, he recognized Parker's black journal was on his desk. Connor was confused because he didn't understand why Parker's journal was in his room. After walking over to the desk and opening the book, he realized that there was writing in it, dated April 5, 2002, which was yesterday. Connor was confused as to why there was writing, because he and Parker both agreed that nothing would be done without Connor coming up with a plan to be followed. However, Connor came to the conclusion that Parker couldn't wait any longer.

Connor understood that Parker had a lot of built-up anger and emotion, but he didn't know that it wasn't controlled. As Connor began reading, he truly felt scared because of the vicious symbolism he used, but at the same time, because of his word choice, he felt as if he was there, just like he asked of Parker to do . . .

Parker wrote,

> As I was lying in bed, reminiscing to myself, I began watching the streetlights beginning to blink two or three times before fully turning on. While I was lying there, I thought, *Why am I in bed right now? I can walk.* Because of that, I decided to sneak out and take a walk down the block, not knowing where I was headed or what I was going to get myself into later that night.

Anyways, I slowly began walking the city blocks, not knowing or thinking about where I was going. As I continued, a man was walking in front of me and began swaying back and forth, as if he was drunk. This gave me the idea to continue following him to see where he was going. He weighed anywhere between 150 and 200 pounds and was at least five foot, nine inches tall. It was hard to tell exactly what colors he was wearing because it was dark and he ended up turning down a back alley, which made it even more difficult to see, but it looked like he had on a blue cut-off t-shirt with brown or black ripped sweatpants.

I really didn't know what I was doing or why I was even following him, but something within me told me to keep following him. As he turned into a back alley, eventually getting between Eighth Avenue and Broadway, it seemed as though he was walking towards the subway station. When he got to the tip of the stairs, without even processing what I was about to do, I lunged at him from behind. As a result, he lost his balance, falling headfirst down the cement steps. I saw him tumbling down the stairs, and for some reason, it felt good. It was like nothing I've ever experienced.

By the time he hit the bottom of the staircase, he was out cold, and from what I saw with my quick glance, his leg was bent behind him, and his arm looked as if it was dislocated. Not to mention, I saw a lot of blood coming out of the side of his head. I didn't know whether he was dead or unconscious, but I guess that's something we could find out in the morning, either on the news or in the newspaper.

Parker finished with,

PS:

Connor, I'm sorry for not waiting to hear your plan, but I couldn't think straight; it kind of just happened.

I guess with us knowing Dad's murderer now and being stuck in this room, I'm going crazy.

I couldn't handle the thoughts that were going on in my head anymore, and I needed to let out some of the anger inside of me . . . I hope you can understand that.

Lastly, it seemed like he was pretty drunk, so it kinda looked like he just lost his balance. I think we'll be fine, bro! Anyway, I love you, man!

As Connor got to the end of Parker's writing, he couldn't believe how much sweat was coming off his forehead and, more surprisingly, the twitches that his muscles were making. He was surprised with the feeling he was experiencing through his brother's words. For some reason, he couldn't get mad at Parker, and it was because even though he didn't wait for one of Connor's plans, Parker still wrote everything down and made Connor feel as if he was truly there.

After settling down, Connor wanted to go find Parker, but he told him to stay away from the hospital, so he didn't know what to do. With Parker out of the picture and Connor not having anyone to hang out with or anything to do, Connor decided to hang low for the day; but for some reason, Connor wasn't feeling too well. His stomach was in knots, and he didn't understand why. The only thing Connor figured was that, with the unexpected morning involving Mr. Harris and his mom dating and Parker's journal, he was mentally and physically drained and just needed a break. With that, he made the decision to stay in bed for the rest of the day.

With Sunday arriving fast and there still being no sign of Parker, Connor decided to go out and look for him. After leaving the house and not really knowing where to start other than the park, Connor decided to look by the subway staircase where the incident happened. Connor believed this was the smartest place to look because he figured that Parker would be trying to replay the other night's scene in his head or, worse, searching for more victims to go after without a well-thought-out plan.

After two hours of searching and with still no sign of Parker, there wasn't much to take out of the day, other than the fact that Connor spotted a lot of victims of his own that he thought would be really good practice for them, particularly Parker. Once Connor got home, he decided to utilize Parker's journal as well, writing,

> All right, Parker, I found the next guy. He's a homeless dude in the park of the East Harlem projects. It seemed like he was walking back and forth on Third Avenue and Lexington. He should stick out; it looked like he hasn't changed his clothes in over a year, so I doubt he'll have anything different on by the time you get to him. I don't really know why I picked this one, but something about him stood out to me, so it led to me following him to his stomping grounds.
>
> Anyways, he has a puffy black jacket on with brown fur around the edge of the hood, with

feathers popping out of the jacket. He's also wearing dark-blue raggedy jeans with a rip in his back left pocket and black Fila shoes. This should help narrow your search down for him, but once you do find him, I want you to follow my plan—and only my plan!

First, I want you to search around the hospital and find chloroform. Then, I want you to get a washcloth and use it to put the chloroform on it. Once you practice that, I want you to find some gloves that you could use that won't rip. When you do those things, I want you to utilize the time that you have to sneak out and become familiar with Third Avenue and Lexington; you need to know this place like the back of your hand. While you're looking around the neighborhood, I want you to find any green Dumpster in one of the alleyways close by; this is where you're going to dump the body.

Second, I want you to attack him at night. You might have to sneak out a little longer than you usually do, but I don't want you doing this during the day.

Now, once you spot him, follow him, but stay out of sight. I don't think he'll realize anyone's following him, but just to be safe, do what I say.

When the time is right and you're about to make your move, you have to make sure that it's close to the Dumpster so you don't have to make extra work for yourself. Trust me, you'll thank me later for all of this planning.

Once this is figured out, sneak up from behind him so that you can utilize the chloroform. Once he passes out, I want you to pull him to the back alley. There's no time for fussing around; this needs to be done quick and effectively.

With this guy in particular, I want you to know that I don't want him suffering. This guy is pretty much a practice run for you. If you can't stab and kill someone while they're out cold, you won't be able to do it when someone's awake and talking. So once he's tied up, I want you to simply get on top of him and do your thing. I don't really care how you do it, but I want it done. You can let me know how you did it when you write it in your journal.

That's pretty much it, Parker. I still can't believe we're doing this, but just be smart, and keep your eyes open. Good luck!

After completing this, Connor felt unbelievable. He didn't know why, but it made him feel as if he was in control of someone's future. With Connor always being in the shadow of Parker and doing whatever people tell or ask of him to do, it seemed as though Connor never experienced this type of power and control. For the first time in his life, Connor was controlling what others do, and more importantly, he was controlling what Parker does.

With school beginning and Connor taking part in his regular classroom activities, ninth period came to a close. Once Connor left the classroom, he took a left and began walking toward the steps, and out of nowhere, José bumped into Connor. At first, they both stared at each other in awkward silence, looking into each other's eyes—Connor, with anger, and José, with a depressed, confused type of look.

Connor did not know what to say, but all he could think about was what he now knew about José and what he deserved. However, with Connor trying to control his built-up emotions, José unexpectedly opened his mouth and began apologizing to Connor. This caught Connor completely off guard and immediately changed Connor's intentions within five seconds— first, because Connor wanted to hurt him, and second, because Connor thought José was still upset with him.

As they began talking and the conversation unfolded, Connor found out a lot. José's dad left his family a few months after the entire bullying incident, and José told Connor that he thinks it was because his dad was embarrassed of José. Once José told Connor this, Connor now understood why things seemed to be different with him. Between the depression disorder being documented under José's file and him being moved into special classes, things began to make more sense.

José wasn't intellectually disabled; he was hurt and had no ambition to do anything. Connor could relate to what José was going through because of what he experienced when he found out his dad and brother died. It is a feeling that completely destructs an individual's thought process—and not only that, but a person's will to live!

By the end of the conversation, Connor felt that he and José never stopped being friends. It seemed as though the wounds were healed and their friendship was back to normal. However, in the back of Connor's mind, he did not know how to act about the entire situation, but all he did know was that it made Connor want to talk to José more.

With the conversation ending quickly due to José unexpectedly having to leave, Connor began thinking, and within three seconds, Parker sneaked up from behind him. Connor was quiet but surprised as to why Parker was there.

As Connor turned around not smiling as he usually does, Parker could tell that something was wrong. Parker asked Connor what was bothering him. Connor replied with "We might have to forget about this vengeance and payback plan." Parker, confused and thrown off guard, immediately replied aggressively with "Why?" Connor explained everything, but he could tell that Parker was incredibly frustrated, and truthfully, Parker didn't care about José or that his dad left. In spite, Parker replied with "Well, now he's experiencing what we have to deal with for our entire lives—a life without a father!"

Connor understood where Parker was coming from, but with Connor being more of the emotional and forgiving brother, he didn't know what to make of the situation. For now, Connor decided to change the subject and brought up Mr. Harris and their mom.

Connor broke the news, and Parker became furious. Due to Parker being in the hospital, he didn't know Larry as well as Connor did, which led to Parker not being able to understand why his mother would do that. Connor explained to Parker, "Mr. Harris has been around a lot since Dad's been gone, and I think he's been helping Mom cope with Dad's death."

"Connor, I don't care what he's been doing. Don't you think it's weird that our teacher is dating our mom? And ironically, he steps into the picture right after Dad's death? I don't know, man. I don't like it."

Connor then looked at Parker with confusion. "So what are you saying? You wanna do something about it?"

"I don't know what I want to do, but I'm fuckin' pissed. Do you have the journal?" Parker asked Connor.

"Of course," Connor replied.

Connor reached into his backpack and handed Parker the journal. Connor, however, didn't like the way Parker was looking at him. He could tell he was pissed, and Connor was afraid that he wasn't going to follow the plan. Connor told Parker, "I wrote everything down in order, so follow it perfectly." Parker looked at Connor with his nostrils flared and barged out of the school.

Chapter 6

Confusion

As the weeks went by and with Connor still trying to balance his plan, he didn't expect things to get as complicated as it was. The more he went to school, the more difficult the whole José situation was becoming. Connor was beginning to enjoy being around José again.

Connor, however, knew that Parker wouldn't approve of him hanging out with José. Connor, at first, didn't plan for them to start hanging out like how they used to, but it seemed as though José was always around, which confused Connor. He didn't understand how José went from never being seen in school for weeks to always being around Connor and his classes, as if he was keeping an eye on Connor.

Connor was happy that he was getting his friend back, but at the same time, the confusion began building up. To make things worse, Parker was in Connor's ear telling him to stay away from José. Parker then brought up a serious point to Connor, saying, "What if José knows what we are trying to do and, by getting

close to you, he knows he can affect your decision-making?"
Connor never thought of that possibility, but at the same time,
he knew that there was no way in hell that José could have
known what they were up to. However, Connor thought, *What
if he's coming up with his own plan, a plan to get back at ~~me and~~
~~Parker~~ for not helping him out during the Jimmy Munn fight?*

Connor was in a predicament that confused the heck out of
him, and he truthfully didn't know what to do. He wanted to
stay away from José, but at the same time, by being around José,
it made him feel that his life was normal again—before his dad's
death or Parker's ~~accident~~. *MISHAP*

Whenever things seemed to get a little easier for Connor,
there was always one thing holding him back. Everything that
was going on was not only affecting Connor's judgment, but he
was now allowing Parker to choose his victims, which would
ultimately result in one of Connor's biggest mistakes.

With this, Parker began to become gruesome with his
murders. He wasn't simply pushing people downstairs anymore,
but now, he was physically executing these people, as if it was a
game. He knew this by reading the journal that Connor asked
Parker to keep so that he would have records of his kills and
how he did them.

Connor reads,

> April 3, 2002
> To tell you the truth, Connor, you're beginning
> to piss me off. I like having a game plan from you,
> a strategy to follow, a mission to complete; it's not

the same without you being in control. You've been off your game lately, but you know what, screw it. You might not like what you read, but this is your fault, so either you start going back to your old ways and our agreement or people are going to suffer more than they have to.

To begin, I will briefly explain what happened with that homeless guy on Lexington. I followed your plan exactly as written, but I did do something that I didn't even know I could do and something that you might not like. You told me not to make him suffer, but things went south. I followed him like you said and waited until nighttime. However, when I went in to make my move with the chloroform, it worked, but I found out within ten to fifteen minutes that I didn't use enough.

As I was beginning to tie him to the Dumpster, he started to wake up. He didn't know what was going on, and it caused him to start yelling. I tried to hold him down so that I could cover his mouth, but he kept throwing me off of him. He began running away, but I caught up to him and leaped onto his back. First, I stabbed him in the shoulder so that he would at least slow down, but all he did was continue yelling. I had no other choice, Connor, other than to slit his throat. I didn't exactly plan to do it this way, but he wouldn't shut up, and I couldn't chance him getting away. I know you didn't want him to suffer, but, Connor, when I tell you it was one of the most exhilarating experiences of my life, I am not lying. The visual image that I experienced and graphic sounds that he was making were like watching a sci-fi movie.

When he finally stopped moving, I dragged him to the Dumpster and was able to get him into it through the side entrance of the Dumpster. He was heavy, but I got the job done!

Now . . .

As for my next victim, I want to introduce you to Elizabeth! This girl was like no other person I've ever met, Connor. I've been keeping an eye on her over the past few weeks and wanted to get familiar with her schedule and surroundings, just like you taught me to do.

Anyways, she came off as a hard worker, but at the same time, all she would do after work is go to the bar and get drunk. I figured she fit our description of a worthless life . . . Well, maybe I was making an exception because of her looks, but we'll get to that.

As Connor was reading, he couldn't believe what Parker was doing. He didn't know what he had planned, and even though the girl didn't really fit their criteria, Connor's heart was beating out of his chest where he could practically hear it pumping.

As Connor continued to read, he could see that Parker was beginning to become extremely descriptive with his writing.

Parker wrote,

> With Friday night in sight and as Elizabeth's walk home from the bar began, I have already prepared the perfect spot to make the kill. With two weeks of following her under my belt, I had her routine down pat, and this made things a lot easier.
>
> As she got out of work on a Friday night and came across the building I was hiding behind, I waited until the traffic light turned green. I did this so that no one from across the street would be able to see or hear me grab her due to the crowded and loud streets of New York City.
>
> To give you a sense of her appearance, she was quite frail, with little arms and limited muscle tone, except for her legs—oh man, Connor, if you can see Elizabeth's legs . . . She also had red hair, dark-brown eyes, and she casually wore red lipstick, which I found rather appealing. I'm not going to lie to you, Connor; I thought this woman was beautiful.
>
> With that, I approached her from behind and grabbed her tightly, pressing her ass against me by squeezing her waist while pushing her as close to me as possible.

With her immediately tensing up, I put one hand over her mouth to silence her scream, and then I aggressively pulled her into the abandoned building and tied her to one of the first-floor banisters. She didn't put up much of a fight. She was surprisingly calm! This took me by surprise, but it did not restrict me from following through with *my* plan.

With her hands wrapped above her head and her body lying there calmly, I began wondering . . . wondering if I wanted to experiment a little bit.

I've been reading a lot lately, Connor, and from the things I've read, many people say that love is a powerful emotion, and when things seem to be going downhill, the love and compassion from someone can make things a lot easier. And with you slowly dissipating from my life and our plan, I think I need more love; I need to feel wanted. I'm sick of feeling alone, Connor, and I think this Liz girl can change that for me.

Connor began sweating and was not sure if he wanted to continue reading. He was afraid that Parker did one of the most inhumane acts on helpless women, and if he did, Connor didn't know if he could ever speak to Parker again. His whole perception of his brother would change in an instant. With the feeling of hopelessness building up within Connor, he knew that he had to read the rest; he needed to know what Parker did to this girl.

Parker wrote,

> As I got closer to her, all she kept asking was "Why are you doing this?" When she asked me that, it really made me think. She actually reminded me as to why we truly started this whole thing. I explained briefly what had happened to Dad and me, and how it has affected our lives and that I was now losing you. This is when she thought she could get inside of my head. She asked, "Do you think that if you do whatever you do with me, it will bring your dad back? I'm sorry, honey, but it isn't." With her saying that, it really helped me put everything that has happened to us recently into perspective. Dad wasn't coming back . . . no matter what! Would he be okay with us doing this? Is this how he raised us?
>
> It began to make me sick what I was doing to this woman and what I have done to others! But then she said, "How about you let me go and I will help you get through this?"
>
> When she said that to me, part of me truly wanted to believe her and have some type of justice come out of this entire situation, but then I remembered that I told her about you and our story. I couldn't take the chance of her going to

the cops and you getting in trouble. Me, I don't really care about, but you, even though you've been betraying our plan, you're still my brother, and I love you.

With that, I made a quick decision; I attacked her—first by holding her down and then by gripping her tightly by her neck. While I looked into her eyes, she looked so beautiful, Connor. With tears beginning to build up on the edges of her eyelids and her being so incredibly scared, I felt a sense of love for this girl. By killing her, I knew it would feel like I lost another person close to me, but losing you, I couldn't afford.

As a result, I reached for my knife. As I gazed into her eyes while she lay there staring back at me, trying not to focus on her trembling lips, the only thing I could say in that moment was "I'm sorry." Quickly after, I pierced my knife into her chest. As I felt the life being sucked out of her, with her heartbeat gradually slowing down, this kill felt like my knife was stuck in her for an eternity.

In that moment, I didn't know what to think. Was this what Dad really would have wanted for us? I kept asking myself that question. Even though the kill felt as if it was relieving some type of pain inside, I still knew this was not the right thing to do.

All of this his might scare you, Connor, but I'm sharing this with you because I want you to know that I need you . . . I need us! I need some control over my life, and without some type of direction, there's no control over what I might do.

As Connor finished reading this, he understood that Parker was going through a lot more than he expected. But even though he was extremely upset with Parker and the way he went about his business, Connor knew that Parker made the right decision to kill her, because they couldn't afford to get caught, especially if they were going to continue with their plan.

Connor knew that he had to figure things out—and fast. He wanted to be friends with José again, but he knew that Parker would not last much longer without Connor on his side.

This was a very tricky situation for Connor to deal with, but he knew that he had to come up with a plan to finally get this entire situation figured out. He couldn't live with his brother acting this way, and the longer he did, the more Connor felt responsible, as if he was the one doing the actual murdering.

With everything going on, Connor knew that he had to try to take his mind off all the negative scenarios that were taking place in his life. With that, Saturday night came around, and Bonnie had her first night off in weeks. As a result, Connor figured that they would be able to enjoy a nice family dinner.

As Connor began making the table, setting up three of everything, Bonnie asked if they were expecting company. With Bonnie not being home much, she wasn't expecting to see Parker. Connor then quickly said, "This spot's for someone special."

Bonnie smiled and looked and Connor. "Baby, I'm happy you set up a plate for Larry, but he isn't coming tonight."

Connor then laughed. "This spot isn't for Larry, Mom." Bonnie looked confused and asked who it was for.

Connor truthfully didn't know if Parker would show up or not, but instead of ruining the surprise, he decided to tell his mother, "I'm not sure if the person is definitely coming, so if they do, you'll be surprised." Bonnie asked Connor if he was having a girl over with a motherly grin. Connor quickly replied with his innocent teenage voice kicking in, "No, Mom."

As dinner concluded and their plates became empty, Connor was upset that Parker never showed up. He felt that it would have been a good surprise not only for Bonnie but for Parker as well. Connor wanted to show Parker that he was always going to be there for him, no matter what. However, because he never showed, Connor was pissed.

As the night unfolded, Bonnie and Connor began to go their separate ways. As Connor walked into his room, he decide to page Parker on his beeper. Even though Parker did not respond, he knew that Parker would get in touch with him sooner or later.

As an hour went by, Connor began getting frustrated, wondering where Parker was and why he didn't answer him.

He was afraid that Parker was taking more murders into his own hands before discussing it with Connor. Connor was still a little shaken up about Parker's last murder, especially because Parker never included where he disposed the body.

As frustration built inside, Parker walked through Connor's bedroom door. Connor jumped up, completely dismissing the fact that he was pissed at him but, instead, wanting to show Bonnie that Parker was here. He grabbed Parker by the hand and told him to follow him.

Connor ran into the living room in excitement but unexpectedly found Bonnie sleeping on the couch. Connor, in disappointment, told Parker, "I guess with this being the first night she's had off in a while, she just wanted to sleep. I'm just mad because we had dinner earlier and I set up an extra plate for you, trying to surprise Mom. I thought it would be nice to have us all together again."

"That was nice of you," said Parker. "I'm sorry I've been kind of distant with you lately. If you read my last entry, you probably know why."

"I understand, bro," Connor replied. "You're going through a tough time, but you should know that I'm always here for you. We're both going through things. We can help each other."

Parker then gave Connor a sympathetic look. "I never thought of it that way. I just didn't know what to do after that last kill," Parker explained.

Connor then said, "Yeah, man, what happened with that? What did you do with her?"

Parker got very serious out of nowhere and told Connor, "Every Sunday, the garbagemen come and pick up the garbage on that street, so what I did was use one of the old rugs in the apartment to roll her up in it then duct-taped the entire thing."

"But won't blood drip out?" Connor asked.

"I thought of that. That's why I wrapped her in contractor bags beforehand, and I also threw her in a garbage container. It's not like the garbagemen are going to pick her up by hand. It's going to be a machine, so we're good. I told you, man, I learned a lot from your planning. That's why if we're going to continue with this thing, I need you."

Connor was impressed but didn't know what to say because even though Parker said he did all these things, he still seemed a little nervous, like he wasn't telling Connor everything.

Connor ended the conversation by telling Parker that he was going to bed. He didn't think he had to direct Parker to his room, unless he was planning on going back to the hospital.

Before Parker closed the door, Connor called out for Parker. When Parker looked back, Connor asked, "How have you been able to get out from the hospital so much?"

Parker explained, "I got close to one of the male nurses over there, and he always covers for me, so I'm good to go. He knows what we've been through, man. I guess he just wants things to get better for us. Anyways, let me worry about that. You keep writing up those plans. Night, man."

The next morning came, and Connor woke up from the sound of someone ringing his doorbell. Connor snapped out of his sleep, not knowing who it could be. Immediately Connor ran into Parker's room, but he was not there. For some reason, he began having a sick feeling in his stomach, thinking something went wrong and the cops were at his door. As a result, Connor tried creeping up to the door. With the knots in his stomach tightening up the closer he got to the door, he then put his eye up to the peephole. Surprisingly, instead of Connor's fear of the police being on the other side of the door, it was a garbageman. Connor didn't understand why there would be a garbageman at his door.

As he opened the door, the garbageman asked if he was Connor Shaww. Connor nodded The garbageman lifted up his arm and said, "I found your book bag on the side of an abandoned building this morning. Here you go, bud. You should stay away from those parts. It's not a good neighborhood." Connor, in confusion, thanked the man and told him that he would keep his advice in mind.

As Connor closed the door, he couldn't figure out why his book bag was there. The only thing he could think of was if Parker borrowed it for something. He then asked himself, *Why would Parker bring my book bag there? Did he need it to carry something? Was he trying to get me caught so he could go through with the plan by himself?*

Connor was incredibly confused, but he was also happy that it was just the garbageman returning his bag and not the cops picking him up for a murder charge. Ironically, Parker walked into the apartment ten minutes after the garbageman left. As soon as Parker walked in, Connor began flipping out.

"Dude, why the fuck was my bag at the building?"

Parker was caught off guard, not knowing what was going on, and asked Connor, "How'd you get that?"

Connor, in a pissed-off voice, explained. "The garbageman just dropped it off. I guess he used one of my books or possibly the journal to find out where we lived . . . Oh my god! The journal! What if he read what was inside? Dude, we're screwed," Connor said in a frightened voice.

"Dude, do you really think he would have shown up here alone without cops or some type of backup if he read what was going on in that journal? Ha ha! I think we're good, man, don't worry. But just to make sure, why don't we make that guy the next victim? We can't chance anything!"

Connor went silent for a split second before saying, "Do you think this is a joke, Parker? This is our life."

Parker then explained, "Exactly, man. We can't take any chances with him going to the cops, so let's take care of him before he has a chance to."

Connor then sat down and began thinking. "I get what you're saying, but he doesn't really fit our criteria. And first off, why was my bag even there?"

Parker began explaining himself. "Yeah, I know he doesn't fit our requirements, but we can't take the chance, bro. We need to complete our ultimate plan. And to tell you the truth, man, a big reason I left last night was to go back and get it. I would have used one of mine, but all of my bags have rips in it from sports, so I needed one that the rope wouldn't fall out of. But I'm happy you got it back, because I almost shit myself when I went to the building and it wasn't there."

Connor was surprised that all this went down without him realizing and then explained to Parker, "Dude, you have to tell me things. I don't care if you use my things, but you have to be more responsible with that type of stuff. That could have been my ass and yours. It's my name in that bag, not yours!"

As Connor was explaining all this to Parker, he could see through Parker's facial expression that he really did feel bad about his mistake and knew that he was wrong. Parker then stood up and told Connor that he was sorry and it wouldn't happen again as he walked out of the apartment.

Connor could tell that Parker felt bad, but he couldn't believe how calm Parker was about all this. This could have been it for them, and Parker acted as though it wasn't a big deal.

Connor was beginning to realize that Parker had no recollection of what they were actually doing and how it could result in permanent jail time. It seemed as though Parker did not care what happened to him as long as the man who killed their father suffered. Connor knew he had to come up with a plan—and quick—because God forbid that garbageman did read the black journal, they would be finished!

CHAPTER 7

How to Fix a Problem

With the Parker problem getting even bigger, Connor had to figure out a solution as fast as possible. Not only was Parker beginning to become reckless with his kills, but also, now he was putting Connor at risk. Connor knew this was becoming a serious issue, but he couldn't afford to stress too much about Parker while that garbageman was still out there. Somehow Connor had to find out who this man was and where he could be found.

As the day went on and Connor began trying to figure out what he was going to do to find information about this guy, he came up with a dangerous but good idea. He planned on walking into the Department of Sanitation building and hacking into their computer system. This would allow him to access information on all individuals who work at specific times for the sanitation company.

With Connor's computer expertise, he felt this should be an easy task for him. The only difficulty that he would face is being able to find the office where he can access this information without getting caught. Connor knew this had to be done quickly, and so he began getting dressed.

Within fifteen minutes of his journey to the Department of Sanitation, he felt as if he was being followed. Connor didn't know why someone would be following him, but the feeling he was getting in the pit of his gut was affecting Connor's thinking. As he got off the bus and walked into the department, he found the door that was titled Staff Directory. However, because it was Sunday, the door was locked. Connor's frustration started to build up, and he didn't know what he was going to do; this couldn't wait. Any longer and it might be the end of him and Parker. With the pit in his stomach getting tighter and the stress building up inside, Connor noticed something in the corner of his eye, and that something was Parker. Luckily enough, it seemed as though it was actually Parker following Connor this whole time, and good thing he was, because Parker knew how to break into locked doors. Before Jeff was a lawyer, he used to work for a locksmith. With that, breaking into locks and doors was something Jeff taught Parker years back. Jeff always told him, "You never know when you'll need to get in somewhere, but don't abuse this talent." Parker took pride in what his dad taught him, and Connor believed that by having to break into the staff directory, it fueled the fire in Parker even more.

Parker, smiling at Connor, pulled out his lock-picking set made up of just two small pins, like paper clips, and began working on the door. Within ten seconds, the door was open, and so was their future. Connor, eager to get going with his search, began hacking into their database. In minutes, he found the schedule for Sunday mornings and looked up the profiles for each employee working during the morning shift and their pickup locations; luckily enough, the personal profiles had pictures of each employee as well. After finding the exact crew that picks up the garbage for that specific abounded building complex, he was able to target the man who knocked on his door; his name was Frank Bergene. Not only was his picture and name under his profile, but his personal address was included as well. Connor knew this would make things a lot easier.

With the stress of finding who the garbageman was coming to a close, Connor knew that his plan had to be written up quickly but executed precisely. He wanted to take advantage of this next kill, specifically for Parker. Connor wanted to enforce an accurate simulation as to how he planned on executing his father's murderer, which would give Parker some practice with how it was going to be done.

After they got the information they needed from the staff directory, both Connor and Parker went their separate ways. Parker went back to the hospital, and Connor headed back home so he could start writing his plan. Once Connor got into his room, he sat at his wooden desk and began writing.

> Okay, Parker, so as you know, we can find Frank at his home address, but in my opinion, I think we should take care of him outside, where we can make it seem as though it was a routine robbery or murder. So what you have to do is

study his everyday routine, as you did with the redhead. After following him for a few days, make sure you figure out where he is going to be on the exact day at an exact time. This is so we can make this work properly. Any screwups and it's our asses.

Once you figure out where you are doing this, I want you to use a different type of blade. I want you to use a *gut hook hunter knife*. The reason you have to use this knife in particular is because this is the type of knife Dad was killed with. I know this because of the video I watched of Dad being murdered, and after doing some research, I found that this was the knife he was stabbed with. If you need money, Mom hides extra cash in her sock drawer. I would never take money from her, but this needs to be perfect. If you decide to do this, come during the day so no one will be home.

Now, I want you to stab Frank with this knife exactly where Dad was stabbed, precisely on the left side of the lower abdomen. You must follow these directions, Parker; I don't want your imagination getting the best of you. We need this man killed quickly and efficiently. The quicker we do this, the quicker we can go after Santiago. Good luck, man. Let's get this done!

With the plan in full effect, the patience of Connor was becoming limited. Connor wanted this guy taken cared of; he didn't want to have to worry anymore about getting caught.

While waiting for Parker to get his directions for Frank, Connor began thinking about the ultimate plan and how they were only one kill away from getting his dad's murderer. Connor knew this was going to be the trickiest one yet. The only true problem that he felt they would face was being able to find Santiago. If his family wasn't able to find him, how was Connor going to figure it out? Just thinking about it caused Connor to get all worked up.

With a few days passing by and Parker trying to figure out Frank's everyday routine, Connor began doing some research of his own. His research consisted of putting pieces together in order to find Santiago. However, during his search, once again, he felt a pit in his stomach, as if someone was watching him again. He figured that the only person who would be following him would be Parker, but even with that, how would Parker have time to follow Connor while he was supposed to be following Frank?

As Connor began walking, heading into the direction of his destination, that pit in his stomach became stronger. He started to believe that he was feeling this way because he was getting closer to where his dad was murdered. Connor wanted to go back to the crime scene to play back the scenario in his head, wondering if it might trigger a memory that he might have missed in the video.

When Connor eventually got there, he decided to sit in front of the ATM. As time passed, he stood up and casually walked over to the side of the building, where he was posted up against the wall. Unexpectedly, a man with the exact same face cover as the man that killed his father pulled Connor into the back of the building. With his hand covering Connor's mouth for him to avoid making any sound, he aggressively said to Connor, "I know what you're doing, and if you don't stop, you'll be next." Connor knew this was Santiago, and Connor tried to get free from Santiago in order to attack him right there and then.

However, with Santiago being a heftier man, he was able to throw Connor to the ground and leave him with a warning. "Remember, I know who you are, but you don't know who I am." Connor immediately wanted to scream out that he knew exactly who this man was, but the moment Santiago put his hand under Connor's mouth, Connor knew where Santiago was hiding out. Connor smelled oil and saw dirt marks on his hands and underneath his fingernails. This ignited a memory that he experienced months back. He remembered that when he and Parker went to José's house for the first time, José told them that his dad was a mechanic, and luckily enough, Connor remembered exactly where José said that his dad worked: "On the corner of Fourth Avenue." Putting two and two together, he figured that Santiago was hiding out there and working so that he could survive on the street. Being the educated teenager that Connor was, he was able to hold back in silence, with the intention of having his ultimate plan working out perfectly.

Once Santiago left, Connor immediately rushed to get back home; he wanted to tell Parker what had happened. Once he got back and saw that Parker wasn't there, he kind of figured that he might be out taking care of business. Connor then decided to do some research on the garage where he assumed Santiago was hiding out. However, he knew that he wasn't going to be able to do this research at home, so he decided to go to the public library so that he can have access to a computer with internet.

Once he got to the library and began his search on the internet, he was able to find the one garage on the corner of Fourth Avenue named Gino's Garage, *"where you bring and we fix!"* Once he found the exact address, he searched their hours. This made it easier for Connor to come up with a time and place where his plan would come into action.

Once Connor found the information he needed, he decided it was time to head back home. On the walk back, he spotted José ironically running across the street. Connor knew it was rare for José to be on this side of the city because he didn't live anywhere near Connor. Connor decided to catch up to him and ask what he was doing over on his side of the city. As he began speaking with José, it was obvious that something was bothering him; José was shaky and seemed as though he was nervous. Connor tried to ask him what was wrong, but all he said was "I'm already late, man. My mom was expecting me home over an hour ago. I have to go."

Connor replied, "All right, man. Be safe."

As José started running away, Connor realized that José was carrying a similar backpack to the one that Connor owned.

Connor thought, *There's no way that's my bag! If it is, that would mean that he broke into my house!* Connor began sprinting back to his apartment complex, where not only was his dog, Baxter, barking, but his apartment door was wide open, as if someone broke into his apartment. Connor immediately ran toward his bedroom and tore it apart, searching for his backpack. He couldn't find it anywhere. Connor knew that if the backpack José had on was actually Connor's, this was a huge problem— not only because the rope was still in it from Parker's last mental breakdown, but also because the black journal was in the side pocket! This would give proof to what Connor and Parker have been up to over the last few months.

Connor had a gut feeling that the book bag José was wearing was actually his and that José was the one who broke into his house. Connor did not understand why José would do this, but because he did, without possibly knowing what he was taking, he left with things that could most definitely make this a bigger issue. With Connor still being in shock, all he could think of was *Santiago must have reached out to José and told him to do some snooping around on us.* Connor became extremely frustrated because things were finally beginning to come together and they were getting closer to going after their father's killer.

As Connor was pacing back and forth within his room, Parker showed up and noticed the facial expression Connor had on. He immediately asked what had happened. Connor explained, and Parker reacted in the same way as Connor did earlier. He was pissed off and didn't understand why José would do this. After Connor gave Parker his belief as to why he believes

José broke in, all Parker could say was "Connor, I told you to be careful with this kid. I knew he was working with his dad, fucking scumbag! His dad's a murderer!"

Connor put his head down, admitting that he was wrong and explained, "The only good thing about this entire situation is that I didn't get the chance to write down the ultimate plan in the journal, so even though he has the journal, he doesn't know what our next move is. However . . . if Santiago reads the journal and wants to end us quick, all he has to do is report us, and we're finished. So all this means is that we have to move fast and kill this motherfucker."

Parker was surprised with how aggressive Connor was acting toward this entire situation and asked if Connor was okay. Connor told Parker, "I'm sick of not being in control, man. Every time I get close to something, it gets taken from me—having to leave Long Island, Dad dying right when our relationship was getting back to normal, and almost you . . . I'm sick of it. I'm going on this hunt with you, and we're gonna finish this guy once and for all." Parker didn't know what to say, but it seemed as though he was proud of Connor and was just as determined to kill Santiago as Connor was.

As the day continued, both Connor and Parker were trying to figure out what exactly they were going to do with José. Originally, he was not part of the plan. Parker, however, made it clear that José was not someone they could trust, and this was proven through his actions of breaking into their home and stealing Connor's backpack. It seemed as though they needed to include José in the ultimate plan. They couldn't take any chances with him. José was already aware of Connor and Parker, and if his dad was to go missing out of nowhere or be found dead, he'd definitely bring the journal to the cops, with plenty of proof to what had taken place during the other murders. It seemed as though José would have to be part of this plan, not because they wanted him to die, but because he left them with no other options. It was time to get this started.

CHAPTER 8

Murder in the First

With school still being in the picture, Connor had to figure out a way to balance school and try to set up the perfect plan to kill someone. With Connor struggling to pay attention in his classes, he began writing the "Ultimate Plan" on a piece of paper. However, with José originally never being part of this plan, Connor was trying to figure out a way to kill two birds with one stone. This was something that Parker never had to deal with, and Connor was trying to make this a highly efficient kill with no mistakes or unexpected scenarios. With it being more than just one person being killed this time, Connor felt that he should split the murders into two separate times and places.

With Connor deciding on this, he also felt that they should take care of José first. This would not only make Santiago suffer with losing someone close to him, as did Connor and Parker, but Connor also believed that it would result in Santiago coming out of his hideout to go after them, which would bring Santiago out of his comfort zone, which was exactly what Connor wanted to happen. This would allow Connor and Parker to plan where they wanted to get targeted so that everything was set up perfectly for their plan to unfold smoothly.

As Connor began writing,

> May 15, 2002
>
> Okay, Parker, this is the plan; we're going after José, and we're going after him now! You're going to go after him at the end of ninth period. I don't want to wait until he and his dad are back together because we've never dealt with killing two people at once. I want this plan to go smoothly with no unexpected fuckups!
>
> Anyways, once ninth period comes around, I want you to track him down and follow him to the south-end staircase where the buses wait for the students. This is when he's going to be at his weakest. As usual, the staircase is going to be packed, and because of that, he's never gonna expect you to take him out.
>
> Now, once he begins walking down the stairs, I want you to squeeze behind people and make this look as if he literally tripped and fell down the steps. You're going to push him, and once you do, you're going to stop and stare, just like everyone else will be! Once this happens and you see for yourself that he isn't moving, then

you can leave. If, for some reason, he's still alive, we'll come up with another plan, but for now, this is how we're gonna get this done! Make this shit happen, man; once you do, we can go after Santiago! Good luck, bro.

After Connor was done writing this, he folded the piece of paper into little squares and put it away into his pocket. Once he did this, he headed toward the bathroom; ironically, José was outside the bathroom staring down Connor, as if he knew something was about to go down. Connor grilled José back with the same intensity, holding himself back with everything he had. With Connor trying to stay under control, he decided to turn around and head back to the classroom. Once he did, he spotted Parker down the hall, which was perfect because he was able to give Parker the note that would give him the plan to take down José.

Parker seemed to be sweating, which resulted in Connor asking what was wrong. All Parker said was "It's done!" Connor was a little confused, not knowing what Parker meant by saying "It's done."

However, Connor knew they didn't have much time and handed Parker the note. Parker asked what the piece of paper was. Connor explained what the note consisted of and eagerly told Parker that this had to be done today. Parker was thrown off as to why today, but Connor made it clear: "The quicker we get this done, the quicker we kill Santiago, and I want this fucker dead, Parker. *Please*, don't ask me again, man." Parker didn't know why Connor was getting so agitated, but he let it slide because he understood what Connor was going through. With their conversation coming to an end, they went their separate ways.

As the school day came to an end, Connor was getting anxious for Parker to get this done. Once he heard the ninth-period bell go off, Connor immediately sprinted toward the south-end staircase. For some reason, once Connor spotted Parker, he instantly zoned out, as if he was the one doing it.

As he watched the moment unfold, Connor was extremely nervous. This was the first time Connor was experiencing someone being murdered right in front of him, and he was in shock. He only read it through the words of Parker, but now, he was experiencing it firsthand.

As Parker waited patiently, he finally saw the red hat that José was wearing that day. With Parker not wanting José to spot him, he put his back toward the crowd as if he was trying to get into his locker, fiddling with a padlock. Once José passed him, he turned around and began to follow him. What José did not know was that his next step was going to be his last, and Connor did not know who was more anxious: him for knowing what was happening or Parker for being the one who was actually doing it.

With José's first step off the staircase becoming closer, Parker decided to make his move. He began creeping behind people, aggressively moving in and out of the crowded students and eventually getting within one person between him and José. This is when Parker decided to take action. As José got to the edge of the staircase and his right foot began to take the first step off, Parker pushed the person in front of him into José, forcing José's body to project headfirst down the steps. However, Parker was able to hold the kid he pushed by the sides of his shirt so that he did not kill someone who did not fit their so-called code.

With the students in the staircase going crazy and people looking at José, the kid who was being held by Parker looked back and knew Parker was the one that pushed him into José. Once Parker saw that José was down for the count, he took off. Parker started running toward Connor, which snapped Connor out of zoning out and immediately led to him running away with Parker. Students began screaming for help, not knowing what else to do. José was not moving, and Parker knew that he was either dead or seriously injured.

As Connor and Parker exited the building, security guards began screaming Connor's name, trying to catch up to them. Connor looked back to see if Parker was behind him, but he was nowhere to be found. Parker went his own way, and Connor felt as if Parker left him to take the blame. Connor continued to run; finally getting out of the school, he then took all the back alleys and shortcuts he knew to get back to his apartment the fastest way possible. Connor knew he had to get his stuff out of his room and fast. If he was being accused for the José incident, he knew that the cops would be coming to his house soon; it was just a matter of time.

Once Connor got into his house, he changed his clothes due to them being drenched in sweat. As he continued to grab his belongings, he was trying to think of some type of plan. Whether it was to sleep on the street or to kill someone for the first time, he was willing to do anything at this point to guarantee his safety and to execute his plan to kill Santiago.

With Parker nowhere to be found, Connor knew he had to take the ultimate plan into his own hands. There was no more Parker in Connor's eyes. He didn't understand why Parker would set him up the way he did, and it pissed Connor off more than anything. With Connor packing his things up as quickly as he could but trying to understand everything that just happened, Parker walked into Connor's room.

All Parker said was "Dude, that was close."

Connor's eyes lit up as if he was ready to burst out in flames, screaming at Parker, "Close? Dickhead! They're blaming me for what happened!"

Parker was confused and didn't understand what he meant. "What? What do you mean they're blaming you?" Parker asked.

"When you left me, I was running, and one of the security guards saw me and knew who I was and screamed my name," Connor explained.

Parker, in denial, asked Connor, "Why didn't you just stay with me?"

Connor was getting more and more pissed by the second and told Parker, "I was running for my life. I never experienced anything like that. I passed you, and I thought you were just following me. I didn't think you were going to leave me!"

Parker then began apologizing. "I'm sorry, man. I wasn't thinking. I just wanted to get out of there."

Connor couldn't put up with Parker's excuses anymore. "I don't care, man. You left me! You're supposed to be my big brother and stick by me no matter what . . . I'm done with you. I'm taking care of Santiago, and that's it!"

Parker took offense to Connor wanting to take the plan into his own hands, screaming at Connor, "In what world do you think you have more of a right to kill Dad's murderer more than me?"

Connor viciously explained, "The moment you dipped out on me was the moment I earned the right to take matters into my own hands. Now get out!"

Parker couldn't believe what Connor was saying to him. Parker told Connor to go screw himself and that he was never going to be able to complete the mission by himself. Parker began screaming at Connor with a sense of pain in his voice, "You don't know what it takes to kill someone!"

Connor, being as confident as he was in that moment, looked at Parker in complete seriousness and said, "Watch me!"

Parker walked out, and Connor was left standing in a puddle of sweat and anger. He didn't know what he was going to do without Parker, but he knew what had to be done, and he was willing to do whatever it took to give his father's death some justice.

CHAPTER 9

Whatever It Takes

Connor was a wreck without Parker, but this was one of the first times in his life that Connor had to depend solely on himself. The time that Parker was in the hospital didn't count in the eyes of Connor. This is because in the back of Connor's mind, he knew Parker was still there, but now, Parker's dead to Connor, and this was a drastic change for Connor to deal with by himself.

With Connor's apartment being out of the question to stay in, Connor needed to find a place and fast. Then, all of a sudden, Connor knew what Parker meant by saying "It's done" He was talking about Frank Bergene, the garbageman. Parker killed him! With Connor remembering the address, he decided that Frank's house would be the perfect place to stay for a night or so, just until Connor could figure out a plan. With that idea in place, he took the chance and walked to Frank's house.

When Connor got to the address, he tried looking through the windows, but it seemed as though every light was off. This directed Connor to the side of the house, where he broke into one of the windows and crawled in. The house was empty, just as Connor anticipated, and so he began his brainstorming.

Connor had a feeling that Parker was going to want to kill Santiago for himself and that he was going to go after him fast. However, because both Connor and Parker were now out of the house, Connor knew that once Santiago found out the bad news about José, he was going to want to go after the boys, and the only person left in the house at night was Bonnie. Connor quickly realized that and instantly knew he had to go back. Then, a little voice in his head told him that he could possibly use this to his advantage.

Connor thought, *What if I camped outside of the apartment building and waited until I saw Santiago go into my apartment complex? Then once he does, I could sneak up on him and make the kill.* Connor felt that this was a good plan and that he could definitely make it work. Even though he was using his mother as bait, he knew that this was the only way he would be able to catch Santiago out of his comfort zone as well as put Connor into his area of expertise. Connor would be at an advantage, and this is exactly what he wanted.

As the day went on and as Connor continued to try to figure out the exact details, he overheard the television. As he turned to watch, he noticed that it was the news, and they were broadcasting live in front of Connor and Parker's school. As the newscaster began speaking, it was titled at the bottom of the screen in bold letters "**Murder at Local High School: José Perez**." With that, Connor knew that if Santiago was watching, he would be moving fast and not wasting any time. What made things worse was that Connor's face was on the news as well. Connor was being targeted as the potential murderer, and the news was trying to put his face out there so that people would report him if he was spotted.

Connor knew that this made things a lot more difficult, such as trying to get back to his apartment complex. With this, he knew that the path back to his house would have to change significantly. He had to stay out of the way of the public so that he was not caught. Connor knew that he was close to accomplishing his goal, and he was not going to let anything or anyone stop him.

With the plan intact, Connor began his journey—first by putting on regular clothes as well as one of Mr. Bergene's hats. He did this because he thought it might act as a good disguise.

As Connor began his mission across New York City, he took plenty of back-alley shortcuts, which added on an additional thirty-five minutes to his apartment complex. However, once he was there, it was around 9:00 p.m. With the sky completely shadowed by darkness and the skyscrapers and streetlights igniting the city sky, Connor was praying that he did not miss Santiago entering his apartment building.

Connor waited patiently in between buildings, pondering what was going to happen when he finally spotted Santiago. With the night passing by, midnight came around, and Connor spotted a man that fit Santiago's description; he was also entering Connor's apartment complex, which finalized Connor's decision to take action and go after him.

As Connor began crossing the street, his blood began boiling, and his anxiety went through the roof. What made things worse was that he spotted Parker following Santiago into the building as well. Connor quickly had mixed feelings about this because he truly had hate for Parker at the moment.

As Connor entered the building trying to catch up to Parker and Santiago, he overhead screaming; however, this scream was not an ordinary scream—it was Bonnie's. Connor raced up the steps, trying to get to his apartment as quickly as possible. When Connor entered his apartment, he saw Santiago standing above his unconscious mother, with Parker nowhere to be found; once again, Connor figured Parker left his mother to save himself.

Connor then jumped onto Santiago's back, pulling him away from Bonnie. As they began wrestling, Santiago was able to grab a lamp and smash it over Connor's head; this loosened Connor's grip and allowed Santiago to throw Connor off him.

Connor, being in shock and not being able to find any type of weapon, then spotted Parker. Parker had the elk gut hook hunter knife and began attacking Santiago. As they began throwing each other into the walls of the apartment, mirrors on the wall began to shatter on the floor. Santiago was then able to punch Parker in the face, which resulted in Parker falling down on the floor. Santiago then began walking toward Bonnie with a piece of glass from the mirror. However, Parker then snapped out of his dazed state and rushed over to Santiago, grabbing him from the back and puncturing his neck with the knife.

Blood began to pour out of his neck, and Santiago fell to his knees, trying to cover his neck with his hands. Unfortunately for him, within seconds, he fell face-first onto the floor, bleeding out almost instantly. Connor, still in shock but conscious to what was going on, began screaming at Parker while walking toward Santiago. Connor then reached for the knife that was pierced on the side of Santiago's neck and started yelling at Parker. "Why the fuck did you kill him? This was my job to do . . ."

Connor, in complete denial, began charging toward Parker with a full head of steam, holding the knife tightly in his right hand, and unexpectedly stabbed Parker in the abdomen. Within seconds, Connor fell to the floor while looking at himself in the shattered mirror. Connor did not understand what had happened. As his vision began to fade, he saw his mother approach him as she asked, "What did you do, Connor?"

CHAPTER 10

Who Is Connor Shaww?

With the morning in sight, Connor was awoken by the sunlightcoming through the hospital window. Connor didn't know what had happened. With IVs coming out of his arms and legs and a bloody bandage wrapped around his abdomen, he did not understand what was going on. This was until his mother walked into his room, where he noticed a sign that said ICU above the doorway.

As the police officers followed Bonnie into the room, Connor could see Mr. Harris in the hallway shaking his head in disappointment. Bonnie sat on Connor's hospital bed and grabbed Connor's hands. With tears coming down her eyes, she was looking at Connor as if she was staring at a stranger. All she said to Connor was "What did I do wrong for you to do this to yourself and so many others, Connor?"

Connor didn't know what to say; all he could get out was "How did I get here, and where's Parker?" Bonnie immediately stood up and pointed to the next room in tears. It was Parker, with an oxygen tube keeping him alive and IVs going in and out of his body.

Bonnie told Connor, "Listen, sweetheart, I understand this has been very hard for you, but you have to listen to me. I'm going to give you the truth. Parker has been in that bed for the past year, not with you, and most definitely not killing people! The cops found your black journal in the back pocket of Santiago's shorts. Why would you do all of these awful things, Connor?"

Connor tried to sit up but was limited due to the pain he was in. He then explained, "It wasn't me, Mom. It was Parker."

Bonnie screamed at Connor, "Parker is in his bed, in a coma! He's been there for over a year! What don't you understand about this?"

Connor was in denial and did not want to accept what he was hearing. Connor did not believe that it was him this whole time. Connor began speaking in a low voice with little hesitation. "I know what Parker and I did, but I'm not taking the full blame for this, Mom! Parker keeps bailing out on me and leaving me with the blame, and that isn't happening anymore."

Bonnie walked over to the police officer and asked for the journal and was able to receive access to it for a few minutes. Bonnie handed the journal to Connor and asked him if he remembered any of this. Connor explained, "Of course, I do. I wrote most of this, but the murdering part was Parker's doing. I asked him to write in the journal when he killed someone so I can feel as if I was there with him. We had a plan to kill Dad's murderer, and we needed to be prepared. But then Parker betrayed me, and things went downhill. I couldn't deal with him anymore, and then when he was the one that stabbed Santiago, I was pissed. That's the reason why I stabbed him."

Bonnie then cut Connor off, screaming, "No, Connor, you didn't stab Parker, you stabbed yourself! That's what I am trying to tell you, that's the reason you're in here!"

Connor went quiet and did not know what to say. Things started to come together, and he began to think back to his last memory. Connor didn't remember getting stabbed by anyone and remembered specifically stabbing Parker, but he also remembered that when he attacked Parker, Parker didn't have anything in his hand to stab Connor back with.

Connor did not know what to say. All he could think was, *Did I really stab myself?*

Bonnie could tell that Connor was confused and extremely sick. Connor began crying, and Bonnie grabbed him, trying to give him some type of comfort. Connor asked if he was allowed to see Parker. Bonnie told Connor that she would have to ask.

As she left the room and asked the doctor if Connor was allowed to do so, she explained that she wanted him to see Parker so that he was able to put things together. The doctor answered, "He is allowed to see Parker, but he must be under police supervision." Bonnie understood and went back into Connor's room and asked him if he definitely wanted to do this. Connor nodded, and the nurses guided Connor into his wheelchair. Connor received a deep stab wound into his abdomen, which resulted in him losing a lot of blood, severely affecting his strength.

As Connor was being pushed into Parker's room, Connor began tearing up. He could not understand what was going on. Parker looked the same as he did when Connor first realized he wasn't dead after the murder of his father. Parker was skinnier, but it seemed as though he never moved. Connor was facing mixed emotions and told his mother, "I don't get it. Why did I see Parker this whole time?"

Bonnie tried to be sympathetic for Connor and explained, "I know things don't make sense right now, but we're going to get you help, I promise!"

As the weeks went on and Connor began his physical and psychological therapy while being under police supervision, he understood what he did. He understood that he was sick and he needed help. In a few days, Connor was going to be entering a courtroom with a lawyer, pleading his case. Connor's lawyer believed that Connor's best chances at a plea deal would be to agree that Connor was and still is battling with psychological disorders known as schizophrenia and multiple personality disorder. By doing this, Connor's lawyer was hoping that instead of going to prison for life for multiple murders, he will instead be put into a psychological facility that helps people battling with the same issues that Connor is living with.

During this stressful time, the weeks have come and gone, building up to the court date. It was evident that throughout the past few weeks, Parker had somehow awoken from his coma. The doctors and specialists that have been treating Parker for over a year did not understand how it was possible, but it was identified as a medical miracle. Connor's lawyer made it clear that Connor would not be informed about this because the doctors were afraid that he would experience a crucial setback from the progression that he made over last few weeks, physically and mentally. With this, the lawyer's plan was to have Parker attend Connor's court case without informing Connor about this. This was with the expectation that Connor would make a scene in front of the jury and judge once he spotted Parker, which would show proof of Connor's psychological disorders.

Even though this was a cruel action by the lawyer and doctors, they knew this was the only way Connor was going to be let off the hook from going to jail for the rest of his life and to get the necessary help that he required.

As the days went by and the day before the court case was upon them, Connor wanted to talk to his mother. When he spoke to her, he began with "Mom, I just wanted to apologize for everything I put you through. Things haven't been easy for either of us, and I know it still kills you that Parker is the way he is, but I promise that I am going to do my best to get better and make you proud."

Bonnie understood that Connor was sick and explained to him, "You don't have to apologize. I understand what you were going through, and just know that I love you very much! We're going to get you the best help possible."

Bonnie wanted to keep Parker out of the conversation because she knew that the shock Connor would be going through shortly was going to set Connor back tremendously.

Chapter 11

New Beginnings?

With Parker being moved out of ICU, he was able to begin rebuilding his strength. With him being out of commission for over a year, he was unable to walk and had limited communication capabilities due to his vocal cords not being used in over a year. Throughout the past few weeks building up to the court case, Parker was getting treatment and going through physical therapy at all hours of the day.

While trying to talk to his mother in a screechy, low-powered voice, he explained, "The hardest thing for me to handle isn't my coma or Dad's death but trying to figure out the thought process that was going through Connor's mind when he was doing all of this. What in his right mind would make him think that I would kill people with him and that it was okay to do this?"

Bonnie explained to Parker, "You have to understand that he's very sick, honey, and with the death of your father and your injury, it caused him to have some type of psychological breakdown. He lost the two most important people in his life and couldn't deal with it. The psychologist said that this is somewhat normal for schizophrenic patients. All we can do is be there for him, but I don't want you to get scared when he sees you for the first time and reacts in a crazy way. It's going to be difficult for him to process everything that is going on and wonder if the situation he's experiencing is actually happening or if it's his schizophrenic mind. It's going to be tough, but you must stay calm at all times."

"I know, Mom. It's just going to be hard. I still have the image of Connor when he was just my nerdy brother that was always trying to impress me. He was my best friend, Mom," Parker explained in a soft, weakened voice.

Parker began tearing up, and it became obvious that this was incredibly hard for him to deal with. He wanted to help Connor, but he understood that the only help he truly needed was medical treatment.

CHAPTER 12

What's Next?

The day was here, and Connor was ready to close this chapter in his life. However, what Connor didn't know was that this final chapter was not yet over.

As court began, a room full of people, as well as news crews, piled in. This court case became statewide news; the reasoning was due to the death of José Perez. This court case was not strictly about him, but it involved multiple other murders that Connor wrote about in his book. With this case becoming some type of big event in the Manhattan area, people were not very fond of Connor at the moment. They did not know that he was sick but instead believed he was going on a killing spree, like some type of serial killer, which he was identified as on the news.

Due to the accusations of Connor being a serial killer, Connor's lawyer, also known as a New York State public defender, opened with a statement addressing Connor's psychological condition.

"Connor is not a serial killer but a sick young man suffering with schizophrenia and multiple personality disorder, and because of these psychological disorders, he made irrational decisions, which unfortunately led to the death of four people."

He also explained why he was experiencing this psychological disorder and what he believed was needed for him in the future so that he could someday be a fully functioning member of society.

With Connor patiently sitting there, quietly trying to hold back his thoughts, the feeling of somebody watching over him crept into his mind once again. Connor tried fighting this feeling because he knew this wasn't real. However, Connor tried turning his body to direct himself away from the jury and judge, and when he looked up, he spotted Parker. Connor stood up and pointed directly at Parker, screaming, "I told you! Mom, look, it's Parker! He's alive! I'm not sick. He's been here the whole time." The court officer immediately ran over to Connor and tried to sit him down, but he continued to plead his case. Things began to get hostile, and Bonnie had to scream at Connor to tell him to sit down. For some reason, throughout this entire process, it seemed as though Bonnie was the only person Connor truly believed anymore.

Connor's mom, sitting beside him, tried grabbing Connor by his face. Once she got control of him, she whispered into his ear, "Parker woke up . . . He is real." Connor went into a fog and began crying. This action immediately showed that he was not in a healthy state of mind. With Connor's actions in court, the lawyer and doctors knew that the jury and judge saw what they needed to see in order for them to understand that Connor needed psychological help and was extremely sick.

With Connor's outbreak, the judge felt that it was necessary to give the victim a half-hour recess, and when court was brought back together, they would have a final decision. Connor was brought back into the courtroom wherein he was being held within a cage, while Bonnie and Parker were outside speaking with the lawyer and doctors.

The lawyer felt that the judge and jury saw exactly what was needed and that it would result in Connor being sentenced to a psychiatric home, where he could receive the treatment that he required. It was a bittersweet moment for the Shawws, but both Parker and Bonnie understood that this was necessary and it needed to be done.

When recess was over and people began filling up the courtroom, they waited for Connor to come back out. The door opened, and Connor walked out in his orange jumpsuit, with shackles wrapped around his feet. As the officer walked in front of him, leading him to his seat, Connor realized that the officer unclipped his gun holster when Connor acted out earlier. As a result, Connor quickly grabbed the security officer's gun and held it toward the crowd. With Connor in full control, he began backing up toward the wall so that he was able to see everyone who was in front of him without a chance of someone sneaking up from behind.

As he held the gun toward the crowd, he began to direct it toward Parker. He began screaming at Parker, "This is your fault! If you never left me alone, none of this would be happening right now." Connor began tearing up and continued with his yelling. "Now I'm in this situation, and there's no way to get out of it . . ."

Connor began wiping the tears that were coming out of his eyes and continued to scream, "I lost Dad then you, and now I'm losing myself! I'm sick of this new life! I'm done!"

Connor then stared at Parker and gave him a wink; Parker, in confusion, did not know what to do. Connor then pulled back the lever and directed the gun toward himself. In that exact moment, life became still for Parker as he witnessed his brother pull the trigger of the gun. The courtroom was in shock, blood was splattered everywhere, and both Parker and Bonnie were devastated. Closest to Connor's body was Parker, and Connor's blood splattered is eyes and mouth. He could taste the bitter, copper-like blood of his brother on his lips, and it was a moment that would be impossible for him to forget. Parker instantly felt that this was his fault, and now his brother was dead because of him.

The courtroom was in panic, not knowing how to react to such an unexpected tragedy. Parker was standing still n the same spot, falling onto his knees, and began shaking. His world, his little brother, was dead. Parker felt as if the world was collapsing upon him. In that moment, he now understood the feeling Connor experienced in that year of loneliness, which led to his psychological breakdown.

Quickly, the cops were called, and the ambulance arrived. People were escorted out of the courtroom, and Parker was forced to leave the premises and his brother's body. With that,

Bonnie saw the effect this incident was having on Parker and was doing her best to be strong for Parker, but the usual sparkle in Parker's eyes was nonexistent.

There was such hope and praise for the future, and now things were torn apart within a split second. Parker felt lost and responsible for everything, and he knew he couldn't do anything to make it better. All he could think of was what Connor was going through in the moments before he killed himself, the feeling of loneliness and emptiness he was experiencing. It was something that Parker never wanted Connor to go through.

Soon after they left the courthouse, Bonnie and Parker made it back to their apartment. The world in Parker's eyes felt empty, as if he was the only person left alive in the entire world, and all he could do was lie on Connor's bed and cry.

While Parker was lying on Connor's bed with his head hanging over the side, Parker saw a piece of paper sticking out from under Connor's bed. It was the folded piece of paper that Connor thought he gave to Parker before murdering José. Parker began reading it, and it made Parker realize that Connor was writing down his emotions and what was going on in his life onto a piece of paper during his schizophrenic breakouts and that his words were just a symbol of how he truly felt inside. This gave Parker an idea.

Parker stepped out of Connor's room, still in disbelief of what had just happened only a few hours ago. He went into the living room to see his mother, but Mr. Harris was comforting her. Parker was still confused as to why Mr. Harris was even around, but these were questions Parker did not care to ask at this point in time. All he did know was that he was not thrilled about having another man around that wasn't his dad or Connor.

Things began to click for Parker. He thought, *So this is what Connor was going through: no Dad, Mom always working, and Mr. Harris becoming the new man of the house.* Parker started to understand why Connor was going through so many emotional and psychological changes. He was under a lot of stress, and without Parker really being there to talk to him, he turned to himself and a made-up Parker.

With Parker needing to get some air to think, he decided to take a walk. As he began walking, he stopped at a corner deli, trying to fill the emptiness in his stomach with food. As he was going down the aisle, he noticed several black journals on the shelves. This brought back memories to the Christmas before they moved from Long Island, when Connor gave Parker a black journal for him to write his emotions and feelings down.

Connor knew that the move was difficult for Parker, and he believed that writing his feelings down into a book and releasing whatever it was that he was feeling would somehow help Parker deal with his problems. Parker had a feeling that maybe if he bought a journal, it would do the exact thing Connor hoped it would. However, in this case, Parker would be trying to figure out a way to deal with the death of Connor, which, as of right now, Parker felt would never go away.

With that in the back of his mind, Parker knew that Connor would have wanted him to utilize a journal during these times, and because of that, Parker decided to purchase the journal.

As he left the deli, he walked back to his apartment and decided to lie down on Connor's bed. Parker slowly opened the journal and took a deep breath. He began writing and titled the first page

The Beginning

June 30

Pl. 8

" 18

" 51

" 57

" 62

" 68

Made in the USA
Middletown, DE
20 October 2017